**The White Star Continuity
Book 3**

CAUGHT

by

Kristin Hardy

The legend continues… With no "out" and no means to reach the outside world, Julia Covington and Alex Spencer are well and truly caught! Trapped in a New York City antiquities museum by a rogue thief isn't the way either of them anticipates spending the weekend, but now that it's happened… What will become of the stolen White Star, the charmed amulet Julia was meant to be researching? And what *won't* they do to amuse one another as the hours tick by?

Dear Reader,

I love new challenges, and when my editor called me about THE WHITE STAR continuity, I said yes practically before she finished talking. I've always found tales of the ancient world to be fascinating, so the whole idea of Batu and Egmath in their desert kingdom caught my imagination immediately. And then when I heard that my heroine was a museum curator, well, I was thrilled. Tracking the White Star through history was a blast—aristocrats, French monks, Roman poets, Greek historians, all on my mental stage as though it were a movie I was watching in my head rather than something I was writing. And getting to go behind the scenes in a world-class art museum was an unexpected bonus.

I hope you'll drop me a line at Kristin@kristinhardy.com and let me know how you liked Julia's story. Of course, by the time you read this, I'll be hard at work on the second half of SEX & THE SUPPER CLUB, available in early 2007. To keep track, sign up for my newsletter at www.kristinhardy.com, where you can also find contests, recipes and updates on my recent and upcoming releases.

Have fun!

Kristin Hardy

CAUGHT
Kristin Hardy

TORONTO • NEW YORK • LONDON
AMSTERDAM • PARIS • SYDNEY • HAMBURG
STOCKHOLM • ATHENS • TOKYO • MILAN • MADRID
PRAGUE • WARSAW • BUDAPEST • AUCKLAND

To Kathryn, for efforts above and beyond the call of duty
And to Stephen
For being pure of heart

Acknowledgments
Thanks to Pamela Hatchfield, conservator, and
Rita Freed, curator of Egyptian art,
Boston Museum of Fine Arts;
and to Robert Burnham,
editor of the Napoleon Series.

ISBN 0-373-79246-8

CAUGHT

Copyright © 2006 by Kristin Lewotsky.

This edition published by arrangement with Harlequin Books S.A.

® and TM are trademarks of the publisher. Trademarks indicated with
® are registered in the United States Patent and Trademark Office, the
Canadian Trade Marks Office and in other countries.

www.eHarlequin.com

Printed in U.S.A.

The Legend Continues

The drums and cymbals sounded. The heavy, musky scent of incense filled the air. Despite the heat outside, the Hall of A Thousand Pillars remained cool with its heavy stone roof and carved columns. It was the Naming Day.

Batu walked along behind her older sister Anan, slowly, matching the pace of her footsteps to the beat of the drums. The cloth of Anan's garments shone white in the flickering torchlight; the gold-and-colored-stone bracelets on her arms gleamed.

Anan had to be exhausted, Batu knew, thinking of the week of ceremonial cleansing, the fasting, the prayers. That morning they'd risen before dawn to go through the rituals, the bathing, the adornments, the dressing of Anan's hair with precious pearls, brought from afar.

It was not every day the ruler of the kingdom was promised her consort.

A throng packed the Hall of A Thousand Pillars, waiting to see the shape of their future. For Anan was not to take merely a husband, but the man who would rule by her side, and from his strength would flow the prosperity and security of the realm.

Batu felt sympathy for her sister, for she knew that Anan's duty was a difficult one. Hers was a life consecrated to the kingdom. How fearful it would be to be in her spot, left without choice, forced to marry the one the priests chose for her.

For Batu was in love.

As she walked, she stared at the dais ahead, at the rich, golden throne, so that she would not look to her side at the line of soldiers guarding their path, so that she would not meet the eyes of the one man she desired above all others.

Egmath. Even the whisper of his name in her thoughts felt like a stolen pleasure. Soon they would tell of their love, soon. But for now, it was theirs to savor, still new in its full flower. When they informed the priests and Anan, it would be a public thing; they would be held separate until they'd married.

And Batu did not think she could bear it.

From the corner of her eye she saw the gleam of the gold cuff around his upper arm. She saw the strong muscles of his chest, the proud carriage of his head. And her heart swelled at the knowledge that this warrior, this man of honor, was hers.

Batu couldn't help it—her eyes flicked toward him to meet his gaze. The rush of it stole her breath. It seemed hardly possible that the love she'd always felt for him had transformed into this tremendous emotion that took her over. This was not the simple affection of children for children.

This was the love of a woman and a man.

Batu followed Anan up the stairs to the dais and moved to stand behind the golden throne as her sister sat. From there, Batu could stare out into the hall, looking at the torchlight flickering off the richly colored pillars. Looking out at the throng that packed the hall.

Looking at Egmath.

On the steps stood Hortath, the eldest priest. At the foot of the dais stood Lagash, the leader of the army, with his soldiers arrayed beyond him. And Egmath by his side.

The music ended, and the silence of the hall was broken only by the rustling of the throng.

Hortath cleared his throat. "May all the gods of this land give strength and health to our ruler, Queen Anan. Let great joy and celebration mark this day, the day the Queen will stand before you with her consort, a great warrior to keep the realm safe and bring forth heirs."

But it wasn't Anan's choice. The priests made the decision, as they did in so many things. Anan would find out at the same time as the rest of the kingdom. She would take Lagash, they'd speculated, though she bore him no love and he was two score harvests older than she. She would take him into her life, take him into her bed.

Batu ached for her sister.

Hortath raised his hands. "Let stand forth the consort whom the gods have chosen." He waited a moment for silence. "Let stand forth Egmath."

And the hall erupted with cheers.

Let stand forth Egmath. The impossible words reverberated in Batu's head. She felt stunned, as though the knowledge held the force of a blow. It was impossible, unbearable. Egmath was hers, her destiny. But the priests wished to control his power and they'd sworn him to Anan.

At the foot of the dais Egmath looked frozen, unable to move. And she who knew him better than all, she who could read every nuance in his expression, saw pure agony in the liquid dark eyes. He looked at her and for a moment they locked eyes, not caring, finally, about the multitudes around them. For a moment, words, feelings flowed through his gaze.

My beloved...

My only...

My lost one...

My duty...

And Egmath stepped forward and strode up to the dais.

TO BE CONTINUED...

Prologue

"I AM SO DONE WITH THIS," Julia Covington said to herself.

And stepped out the door into thin air.

Not surprisingly, she dropped like a rock. That was why smart people knew enough to stay *inside* the airplane.

They'd lied when they'd said it was like flying. It wasn't a bit like flying. Or floating. What it was like was falling, strapped to a jump instructor, her stomach up her throat, the wind flapping around her, nothing to hold her as she watched the distant—and really large, really hard—earth come inexorably closer.

And her mind, analytical to the last, couldn't stop processing. Acceleration due to gravity was thirty-two feet per second squared, which meant every second she fell thirty-two feet per second faster. Until terminal velocity, of course, a mere hundred and twenty miles an hour, which she should be reaching shortly. On the ground she'd get thrown in jail for going a hundred and twenty miles an hour. Up here she just got charged a lot of money for the privilege. A hundred and twenty miles an hour—more than sufficient to make a nice little splat when she hit the ground.

She really hoped she'd packed the parachute right.

She glowered at her old college roommate Sasha, who'd come up with the whole extreme-sports idea. *It'll be good for you. Live life on the edge.* Grinning giddily, Sasha waved.

"How did I let you talk me into this?" Julia shouted, words that were ripped away by the wind.

Sasha cupped one hand to her pressure helmet. "Whaaat?"

Julia shook her head. It didn't matter. She knew why she'd done it—the same reason behind nearly every absurd thing she'd done over the past eight months. Since her divorce. Since her emancipation from Edward Cleary, her controlling, disillusioned Svengali of an ex-husband. Edward, who'd loved her as the naive student he could mold and instruct. Edward, who wasn't at all prepared for a Julia with a mind of her own.

And she'd been demonstrating that mind of her own since the papers had been signed by trying every foolish thing she could think of that would make Edward turn purple with disapproval. So okay, maybe the incident on the balcony at Mardi Gras hadn't been well thought through, but she'd crash the Miramax party at Cannes again any day.

It had been a pretty fun eight months.

And it was time to end it.

Too bad she hadn't come to that decision before she'd leaped from the airplane. Timing, as they said, was everything.

She felt the tap of the jump instructor on her shoulder and she swallowed. The minute of free fall had whipped by astonishingly quickly. Now came the moment of truth, the moment she pulled the rip cord. A featherlight landing or…splat?

Julia grasped the toggle. She stared at the ground, at the squares and circles of green rushing toward her. What was the saying—God protects fools and drunks? Well, she certainly wasn't drunk, more was the pity, but she was the champion of all fools.

Holding her breath, she tugged—

And with a whispering rush, the chute unfolded smoothly, dragging her vertical. Suddenly, she was floating, with the world spread out below her. Okay, now this part wasn't so bad. This, she could do. Now she had time to think, time out from the world to figure out what came next. Because she was going to be hitting ground eventually, and when she did, it was time for a change. Most women had transitional men after divorces.

She'd had a transitional life.

Time to move on. Of course, she'd had a transitional man, too—or at least a transitional purely sexual, as-often-and-outrageous-as-possible affair. She sighed wistfully.

Time to move on there, too.

Because when you came right down to it, she wasn't wild Julia, skydiving, sex-in-public party girl. She was serious, practical, collected Julia. Anything else was temporary, a pose.

The past five minutes had graphically demonstrated that to her.

It was time to get her life back in order. When she hit the ground, she'd get started. When she hit the ground, it was time to make some changes.

1

"GOOD LORD." Alex Spencer rolled onto his back, gasping for breath, heart hammering against his chest. "No more Asian sex manuals for you, woman. You've ruined me."

"*I've* ruined you?" Julia Covington managed through her own heavy breathing.

With her dark hair tumbled loose and wild around her shoulders and her skin gleaming pale in the light from her entryway, she looked like some odalisque in a seventeenth-century painting—beautiful, tempting and thoroughly addictive. Even now, looking at her made him dry-mouthed with desire.

If he'd been thinking straight, he'd have been worried.

Then again, he'd hardly thought straight once since that evening she'd appeared at the museum fund-raiser in a flame-hot red dress that had left nothing to the imagination. The dry, serious Ms. Covington, who never appeared in anything but utterly simple garments in shades of taupe, charcoal and cocoa, was suddenly a siren. He couldn't have said what had shocked him more—the dress or the fact that she'd left with him.

And every moment since had pretty much been a toss-up.

"Yes," he murmured against her mouth, "you've ruined me, milked me dry, left me a worn-out husk, old before my time."

He could feel her smile. "I had some help with that, I think. Some very enthusiastic help."

He worked his way down her throat, feeling the first faint stirrings of arousal yet again. "Come on, what do you expect a guy to do when you show up at the door in nothing but a robe?"

"What was I supposed to be wearing at eleven-thirty at night?" she said and caught her breath. "You were lucky I let you in at all."

He smiled beatifically. "I got lucky, all right." He moved his hands and felt her quiver in response. "And if you give me a minute or two, I just might be in a position to demonstrate my appreciation."

"Well, you'd better do it quickly, Lothario," she said— a little unevenly, he noted in satisfaction. "I have to get to sleep. I've got work tomorrow—today," she corrected after a glance at the mantel clock. "Something you might want to think about, also." She shifted away from him.

Alex calculated and tried for pitiful. "I spend four days in D.C. fighting the sharks for NEA funding, and you're throwing me out?"

It didn't work. "You told me last week it was going to be a schmoozefest where the most challenging thing you'd have to do was drink champagne and eat crab claws."

"And you think that's easy?" he demanded.

Julia just snorted and rolled to her feet, plucking her Chinese silk robe off the living room carpet as she rose. "Nobody made you come here, you know. You didn't even call to warn me."

And, as always, the minute they stopped touching, brisk, matter-of-fact Julia came back.

"I thought you women thought spontaneity was romantic."

"We're not having a romance," she reminded him firmly as she tied the belt of the robe. Too firmly.

"Oh yeah, right. No relationship, no talking, just sex." Alex reached for his trousers, pushed down the little surge of annoyance.

"Exactly. You sales types should know better than to try to renegotiate as you go along."

"Marketing, not sales," he corrected. "We don't sell antiquities at the museum." He stopped in the act of buttoning his shirt. "Unless you've got a sideline I don't know about. In which case, we'll have to find out whether they give conjugal visits to lovers."

She frowned. "We're not lovers."

"Right. If we were lovers, I'd be going to your bed right now instead of getting kicked out into the hall." Even he could hear the edge in his voice. "I came here because I missed you." He'd come because he couldn't make himself wait until the next day to see her. "You were off with your skydiving thing last weekend and then I was gone. It's just been a while. I thought you might miss me."

Julia got that countess look he'd learned she put on when she felt she was losing control of a situation. She handed him his shoes. "Alex, it was nice to see you, really. But it's late." Her voice was brisk. "We're getting together tomorrow night anyway."

"Good, because I think we should talk about this."

Relief flashed into her eyes, a relief that made him wonder. "Good. I want to talk, too. But it's late and I'm tired and husks like you need your sleep. You should go."

And then he was standing out in the hall, garment bag

and jacket in his hand, staring back at the door that was closed to him.

Like Julia.

JULIA SAT IN HER OFFICE at the New York Museum of Antiquities, staring out the window past the enormous pillar that obscured half her view of Fifth Avenue beyond.

Alex Spencer. The good-looking charmer, the golden boy who succeeded at everything he touched, always a nice word for everyone. Always somehow sensing when she'd been down during the worst of times with Edward, making her laugh with a joke even though she'd said nothing to anyone about how she was feeling. It had been temporary insanity the day of the museum gala six months before when she'd bought that outrageous dress purely because it would have appalled Edward. It had been temporary insanity that had made her wear it to the gala and definitely temporary insanity that had had her leaving with Alex Spencer.

She'd quite clearly been out of her mind.

That was probably why the sex had seemed so amazing, just as the skydiving might have been amazing if she'd been in the right mood.

Or maybe not.

All right, bad example. Luck, that was it. It was just pure luck that Alex happened to have an instinct for how to touch her. It was just that charm monster thing he had going that always made her feel so good around him. After all, it wasn't as though they had a relationship or anything. They had zero in common except sex.

Anyway, they'd rarely managed to get out even basic pleasantries before ripping one another's clothes off most times, which suited her to a T. If she had to talk to Alex Spencer, she'd be forced to face how wrong, how ridiculous, how brainless she'd be to think of them as a match. The way she'd been with him, that wasn't her. That was the artificial post-divorce giddiness. The real Julia was quiet, sedate and studious.

The real Julia was someone Alex Spencer wouldn't give a second glance.

Which was fine with her, she thought quickly, because he wasn't her thing, either, any more than public indecency at Mardi Gras was. She wanted a man who was serious, focused, someone who was an achiever, not a fun-loving, slick G-boy with no sense of propriety. Thinking of the chances the two of them had taken together made her squeeze her eyes closed.

Thinking of the chances the two of them had taken left her awash in lust.

She made an impatient noise. It was time to end their little arrangement, no matter how much fun it was. She was ready, finally, to go forward with her life, and that life didn't—couldn't—include Alex Spencer.

Putting Alex firmly out of her mind, Julia flipped through the latest issue of *American Curator.* A major auction of early Roman pieces was scheduled for fall, she saw, making a note to herself. Some recent reports of ancient Egyptian and Babylonian forgeries. And a story about the heist of the Zander collection from Stanhope's Auction House. No leads there.

Reading the list of items taken was enough to make Julia's eyes cross well before the end. A shame, but having met Zoey Zander at a few of her mother's society dos, Julia would have laid even money that the "antique" items weren't even authentic. The jewels, perhaps, but as for the rest of it, Zoey was more about flash than substance. Having it look right was more important than having it *be* right.

Julia had never understood that. To her, it was the history of a thing that mattered, the story she felt when she touched it. Absently, she rubbed a finger over the bit of scrimshaw that sat by her telephone, a personal treasure that she knew she shouldn't touch with bare hands but was helpless not to. She could imagine the whaler who'd spent long, windblown days working at the ivory, setting it aside at the cry of "Whale ho." If she closed her eyes, she could smell the salt tang of the sea, feel the motion of the ship, imagine the distant blue horizon and the pale vault of the sky overhead.

It had always been like that for her, since she'd been a child. She remembered going to the Metropolitan and staring at a pale blue glass cup in the antiquities wing, a glass that had been in the ground so long it had turned iridescent. It fascinated her so much she'd relentlessly pestered her mother, her nanny, her great-aunt Stella to take her to the Met over and over. *An artifact from an ancient desert kingdom,* she'd read on the identification card and imagined a little girl like herself who might have drunk from it. And at night, she'd dreamed that she was the little girl, a princess whispering in the desert dusk with her favorite friend, a young boy who dreamed of becoming a great warrior.

She hadn't had that dream for a long while.

"Hey, gorgeous."

No matter how wrong for her he might be, something about Alex's voice always sent a warm shiver through her, whatever she was thinking, whatever she was doing. Julia opened her eyes and gave her visitor a bland look. "Well, if it isn't the infamous Alex Spencer."

He leaned against her doorway, looking like some *GQ* model in his expensive suit and hand-dyed silk tie. "Miss me?"

She rolled her eyes. "How can I miss you when you won't go away?"

"I can't go away. I have to stick around to keep you from falling asleep at your desk." He clicked his tongue at her. "Maybe if you got to bed at a decent hour, you'd be more awake."

"Sometimes I get pestered by late-night callers," she said.

"You shouldn't answer the door, then."

"I'll remember that next time." She folded her hands in front of her. "So what can I do for you, Mr. Spencer?"

"A favor." He stepped into the office and her lungs took a breath of their own accord. Honestly, there was nothing the man could do that wouldn't look good. He had a gift for it, from his cropped dark hair spiked with just a bit of gel to his glossy Italian leather shoes. And she knew from personal experience that he looked just as effortlessly handsome in shorts and a polo shirt.

Or in nothing at all.

Maybe it was the thousand-watt smile, the square jaw, those green, green eyes. Eyes currently glimmering at her in humor, making her realize she'd been staring far too long. "Making notes for a portrait?" he asked.

"Wondering if I maybe saw you on the post office wall," she replied. "So what's the favor?"

"Someone I want you to see today. My sister's got a friend who wants to bring in something for you to look at. She thinks it might be valuable—"

"Alex, no," Julia was groaning before he'd even finished. "No, no, no. You know how it works. They've gone to a flea market or on holiday to Morocco and they've got some piece of trash they're convinced is the real thing."

"Maybe it is," he suggested.

"And maybe it's a tourist tchotchke. Do you have any idea how often I've looked at those kinds of things?" she pleaded. "They're never real. Trust me, antiquities don't just fall in a person's lap." But he had that gleam in his eye that he always got when he proposed something outrageous, she saw sinkingly, that look that always seemed to get her to do what he wanted.

"Look, it's a favor for my sister. Why don't you just give it a look and see what you think?"

"I have a better idea," Julia said silkily. "Why don't *you* look at it?"

"I've got to leave for lunch with a big donor—" he glanced at his sleek Bulova "—like, right now."

"And I've got meetings all afternoon."

"Then it's good she's coming this morning, isn't it?"

That stopped her for a moment. "Well, aren't we sure of ourselves," she said tartly.

"Oh, come on, Julia, it's five minutes. It's for my sister. Family."

And if she didn't watch it, she'd cave to him yet again, just as she had the night before. With everyone else she was intelligent, self-possessed, in control. It was only with Alex that she lost the ability to say anything but yes. "I don't have time," she lied. "I don't know what made you think I'd agree."

Alex stepped inside and closed the heavy wooden door. "Maybe I could offer you something in return." He ambled across the room looking amused, as though he could read her like the Sunday *Post*.

"What do you think you're doing?" she asked uneasily, already feeling the treacherous flutter in her stomach.

He didn't answer, just leaned on the corner of her desk. "You know that your eyes always get a little darker when I come close?" he asked conversationally, reaching out to take her hand. "And they definitely get darker when I do this," he added, touching the tip of his tongue to her palm.

And lust just exploded through her. For an instant, all she wanted was to have him naked, against her, on top of her. In her. Outside in the hallway, voices passed by the door, chattering about the weekend.

Inside, Julia froze, mesmerized by a touch, staring, boneless. And she'd just sat there and let him do it, she thought in annoyance. She wasn't the type to just melt because some good-looking guy stroked his thumb over the back of her hand, stroked it and stared at her and made her think of what else those hands could do....

"Stop it." She rose hastily. "We're at work, remember?" And if she didn't get at least a few feet away from him, she wouldn't care.

"Forget it." Alex stood and circled around the desk toward her, easy, relaxed, making her think of one of those clever, nimble border collies. Which, she supposed, made her the sheep. "Look, the door's closed. And it's not like I'm planting one on you, as much as I'd like to," he added, approaching her. Julia took a few wary steps away. "Anyway, who's going to care? It's not like we work in the same department."

"Wait a minute. I care." She held on to the sudden flare of anger like a shield. "I'm not going to be the latest watercooler topic."

He grinned. "Sweetheart, if people haven't figured out there's something between us by now, they're blind."

Sweetheart. He had no right to use the word to snatch the breath from her lungs. "Well, they're behind the times, because there's nothing between us," she snapped. "It's over, all right? Done."

Alex blinked. "What are you talking about?"

"Us. This...*thing* we've been having," she said, throwing her hands in frustration. "I was out of my mind to start it, I've been out of my mind to keep it going and now I'm finished. Want me to be any clearer? I want you out of my *life.*"

She'd never seen Alex in anything but easy good humor, so it took her a moment to realize he was angry. "Where's this coming from? You don't just come out of nowhere and cut it off."

"I'll do whatever I want to."

"You said we were going to talk tonight."

"I'm done talking," she flared.

He rounded on her. "That's right, you don't talk, do you? No talk, just sex. Don't get to know each other, don't find out about each other's lives, just get together to scratch an itch. Well you know what, Julia? That's a crock of—"

A knock on the door interrupted his furious words. For a breathless instant neither of them moved. Then Julia smoothed her trim claret suit and walked over to open the door. "Yes?"

She saw a couple outside, the woman looking tense, the man clasping her hand protectively. "Are you Julia Covington?" the woman asked.

Julia nodded.

"I'm Marissa Suarez. This is my...boyfriend, Jamie Wilson. Alex Spencer said you'd be expecting us."

Alex stepped up behind Julia and the hairs on the back of her neck rose as though in a field of static electricity.

"I'm Alex," he said, stepping around her to put out his hand to shake. "Nice to meet you both. Unfortunately I'm late for a lunch appointment, so I'll have to leave you in Julia's hands." Only Julia would have seen the spark in his eyes. "I'm sure she'll be happy to talk with you. Julia's always happy to talk with anyone."

JEAN LUC ALLARD walked into the museum, sneering inwardly at the guard who stood at the front door. So tall, so cocky in his uniform, with his gun. Pathetic. He could no more block a professional like Jean from his desires than could a child.

It was always so. Those who were robbed were the weak. He was one of the strong. No one bullied him, not since he'd become a man. Not since he'd left his whoreson of a father crumpled and bleeding in that Marseilles alley, maybe dead, maybe alive. Jean neither knew nor cared, as his father had never cared all the times he'd treated him like so much filth beneath his feet. It was a debt paid, nothing more.

Jean took what he wanted and prospered. After all, there was always a market for a man with certain…talents. His clients knew how to find him, and he knew how to get them what they wished.

Like the White Star amulet.

So beautiful, so alluring, a treasure that demanded to be touched. A seductive beauty that did not easily release the mind. When he'd sat across from his contact in the dark corner of that Parisian tavern, he'd been given only a description, a location, a name. Now that he had seen her, he knew what she could drive a man to do. He knew what a man might do to possess her.

And he knew his client would pay more.

All he needed to do was retrieve her from the foolish Suarez woman. Perhaps she had been lucky since he'd been forced to place the amulet in her bag to avoid detection, but it was of no matter. He had been punished for his foolishness, and now it was at an end. The White Star was his to take.

He walked down the hallway with its echoing marble walls. Friday midday and all the little people had scuttled out of their cramped offices for lunch before their afternoon of meaningless rote work, like rats on the wheel. Pah. Fools, all of them, laboring their lives away for nothing, telling themselves they had control, deluding themselves they had security when he could move among them at will and take whatever he wanted.

And what he wanted, he thought, listening to the voices inside the open office door, was his White Star.

2

"PLEASE, SIT DOWN," Julia said, waving Marissa and Jamie to seats before she crossed to her own chair.

"Thank you for agreeing to see us," Marissa said. "I'm sorry we interrupted you."

"It was nothing." Julia welcomed the distraction. It let her heart level. It kept her from thinking about the look in Alex's eyes. Instead, she studied the couple sitting across from her. For they were a couple—she would have known it before Marissa had said a thing. It wasn't the clasped hands, but something that hummed between them, something that tied them as surely as a physical bond.

She wouldn't have put them together at a glance. Marissa looked too polished, too fiery for Jamie's slightly rumpled, abstracted air. They seemed…glowing, somehow, though. Connected.

Shrugging the thought aside, Julia folded her hands. "So," she said briskly, "what have you got?"

The two of them exchanged glances. Marissa moistened her lips. "I was just on vacation," she began. "I wound up with something, and…"

Ah, the dreaded vacation find, Julia thought in resignation, but then she realized there was a tension about

Marissa, a strain in her liquid dark eyes that didn't bespeak a flea-market tchotchke. "And?" she prompted.

"Look," Jamie broke in. "How about if we don't tell you anything about it. Just…look at it. Tell us what you think. Tell us if you think it's real." He turned to Marissa. "Okay?"

She nodded and opened up the leather bag she wore strapped across her chest. Reaching inside, she brought out an object wrapped in cloth and laid it carefully on the desktop before unwrapping it.

And Julia felt the unholy punch of excitement in her gut. This wasn't a vacation find brought in by some poor, deluded soul. This was the real thing. Where it had come from or how it had gotten there, she couldn't say, but she could sense the power of its age as though it were radiating waves of antiquity.

It wasn't colored as so many of the pieces of that time were, and yet she was as certain as she was of her own name that it was ancient. Thin veins of gold chased around the carved ivory, an ivory so white despite the years that it seemed to radiate somehow. It was shaped like a star, with a hole through the center. Looking closer, she saw shallow etching, so faint and small as to be almost invisible, worn away, perhaps, by the years. Gods, designed to carry the bearer to the afterlife?

Julia rummaged blindly in the desk drawer for the wooden box that held her loupe, unable to take her eyes off the piece. Who had carved it long ago, sitting in some dusty desert workshop, never guessing that his handiwork would leap across centuries, millennia? What had it meant? What power had he believed it held? Slipping the loupe in place, she looked closer.

Only to be astounded by the detail. The figures stood facing one another, hands clasped. A man, a woman, staring into each other's eyes. In each of their breasts a tiny dot of embedded carnelian flamed red, seeming almost to pulse before her eyes. And the hairs prickled on the back of her neck.

Not gods. Lovers.

A ribbon had been strung through a faceted hole that pierced the amulet just below the joined hands. "Have you been wearing this?" Julia asked, glancing up.

Only to see Marissa's cheeks tinting. "Only once," she said, refusing to look at her boyfriend. "Before I realized it might be valuable. Is it?"

"At a glance I'd say it's possible, but I'd have to spend more time looking at it." Caution was the way to go. As certain as Julia felt, she'd seen the best and brightest fooled by clever forgeries. The article in her magazine just that day had detailed more than a few instances where shady dealers had profited. Something else nibbled at the edge of her memory. "Could you leave it here with me for a day or two?" she asked impulsively.

"But we—" Marissa objected.

"Hold on," Jamie said to her. "It might be the safest place for it. Keep anything unexpected from happening to it." He stared at Marissa intently and some message passed between them. "How is your security here?" he asked, turning to Julia.

She blinked. "The best. Why?"

"Just want to be sure it's protected," he said affably.

"We've got twenty-four-hour guards, electric eyes, motion detectors, the whole deal. The amulet will stay locked in my office safe unless I'm working with it. It looks familiar. I've got some source texts downstairs I want to consult."

"We think it might be the White Star amulet," Marissa blurted.

That was it. Stolen from Zoey Zander's collection, Julia realized. But that heist had been carried out by professionals. She frowned. "Why haven't you gone to the police?"

Marissa flushed. "We wanted to be sure it was real," she explained. "You have to admit, it seems pretty unlikely."

Certainly they looked like the unlikeliest of thieves. Then again, the best thieves did. "How did you come by it?"

"The guy who stole it might have dumped it in Marissa's bag at the airport. We think we've seen him," Jamie added.

Which explained the questions about security. And the strain. Then again, the strain could have stemmed from taking a criminal risk.

"What do you think?" Marissa asked.

Julia looked down at the amulet, the lovers frozen hand in hand. The White Star. There were legends, she remembered vaguely, something fanciful about true love. "It's possible," she allowed. "But you have to understand, even if it is the Zander piece, it may not necessarily be the real White Star. It's very difficult to authenticate antiquities, especially if the forgery itself is an antique."

"But it was being auctioned off," Marissa protested.

"Even the best experts aren't infallible," Julia said wryly. "We can all be taken in. Leave it with me for a few days. I'll take some time to look it over, check to see if I can find anything definitive to authenticate it." And if it *were* the real White Star, she could get the police involved.

"Whatever you can do," Jamie said and rose.

Marissa stood and reached out a hand longingly toward the amulet but stopped short of touching it. "It's so beautiful," she murmured. "I don't care if it's real or not."

"If it is the White Star, it's not ours," Jamie said

gently, putting an arm around her shoulders. "We only got to borrow it for a little while."

And to Julia's everlasting shock, Marissa laughed and threw her arms around Jamie's neck and gave him a kiss hot enough to vaporize metal. "And honey, we made the most of it."

FOOLISH WOMAN, to boast of security. As though motion detectors and pressure plates could keep him out. As though a mere office safe could block him from his prize. The White Star was his in all but actual fact. It was but a matter of time.

He itched to hold her again. It was maddening to have her so close, yet out of his grasp.

But he was a patient man.

For now, hovering in the gallery near the entrance to the office wing held the most promise. He could linger, invisible to the imbecile guards, and watch. It was, after all, a museum, a place designed for lingering. He would bide his time, learn what he could. He could wait as long as he needed.

And when night fell, he would strike.

HELL, JULIA THOUGHT wearily at day's end, probably bore a lot of resemblance to the twelve-person, three-time-zone telecon she'd just suffered through. There was nothing like trying to pull off a tricky negotiation with a host of stakeholders, none of whom you could see. Foolishly, naively, she'd assumed that because everyone stood to benefit from the multimuseum traveling exhibit she was hoping to pull together for early 2008, they'd all cooperate. Ha. Throw in egos, tempers and language barriers, and you had a recipe for chaos.

Meanwhile, she'd been almost entirely unable to keep

her mind from drifting back to the amulet. And to Alex. Things with Alex were over, she reminded herself. She should put him out of her mind. The amulet, however…

The shadows outside had grown long by the time she spun the dial of her safe and drew out the unadorned wooden instrument box that held the amulet. It was the box that usually cradled her loupe, but she'd switched it for the Suarez woman's piece earlier that day. Her loupe would do just fine unprotected for a short while. A three-thousand-year-old ivory amulet—if it was indeed the White Star—wouldn't.

Julia put down a padded mat on her desk and laid out the amulet. She wouldn't allow herself to think of it as the White Star, not until—unless—she demonstrated its provenance. That was her task. That was her challenge. But for a moment, just a moment, she let herself look. And with her hands freshly washed to remove all possible contaminants, she gave herself guilty permission to touch.

Power, warmth hummed up her arm.

She was a scholar, an educated woman with a disciplined mind. Hocus-pocus made her impatient, but her secret, the thing she told no one, was that she could feel something in the truly ancient objects, something beyond what her trained eye could see, beyond what her educated mind could know. There was some connection she made with the past.

And she could feel it in the amulet, stronger than she'd ever felt before. She felt age, hot desert air, the whisper of sand. And a bittersweet mix of love and sadness that had her jerking her hands away.

After a moment she shook her head. That was what she got for being ridiculous. She knew what she needed to do, Julia thought, snapping on gloves. Characterize, compare, research, document.

The fundamental steps to authentication all began with a physical record, of course. Digging out her digital camera, she began snapping photographs of the piece from every angle. Annie Leibovitz, she wasn't, in oh so many ways. The very paleness of the ivory foiled her every effort; even with the light dimmed, she couldn't capture the carvings. So she got out a pencil and paper and began to make a set of careful, painstaking drawings, studying the amulet through the loupe, front and back, from every side, recording every possible detail. Okay, so she wasn't da Vinci, either, but at least she finished up with a detailed record.

Finally, she put the amulet into the box and rose. Characterize, compare, research, document. She already knew the museum had nothing precisely like it, which eliminated the need to compare. Time to get on to part three.

In the hall, she heard the familiar end-of-day sounds of people closing up shop and going home. For her, it was time to get to work.

"Hi, John," she said to a passing security guard as she exited the office wing into the Mesopotamian gallery.

"Where are you going?" he asked. "It's quitting time. Time to go home."

"Is that why everyone's been leaving every night?" She laughed and took the unobtrusive door that led down the stairs to the basement level, headed for the conservation lab and its rare-book repository, her favorite place in the whole museum.

She'd always loved books, from the time she'd been little. The day she'd seen her first truly old book, though, she'd felt a deeper excitement. There was something magical about holding a volume that had been labored over a thousand years before or a scroll written by a man long since dust, something that fascinated. There were secrets in the leather-bound tomes from centuries gone by, mysteries in the scrolls of papyrus and parchment. And now, she was on the ultimate bigger-or-better hunt, hoping to find a trail of clues that would lead her back through the ages.

Hoping to find the story of the White Star.

She had help. An indexing project a decade before had produced an electronic card catalog of the materials in the library, with summaries, chapter heads, even main topics covered. There was no substitute for the real thing, though, for the rich gleam of illuminated manuscripts, the careful script of the Greek codices, the writings of Pliny, Clio, Herodotus.

As she hit the crash bar of the door to the basement level and turned into the hall, she heard the tread of feet above her. Someone doubtlessly headed home from upstairs, she thought. Friday night, the time to meet friends for drinks, go to a club, relax. The museum was quieting, all the visitors gone and the staff quick to follow.

It was her favorite time.

The rapid tap of her heels rang in the hall. The museum's Gilded Age founders had spared no expense in the construction of the building, even down here. Veined marble walls soared up to nine-foot ceilings. The ornate locks and hinges on the solid-oak doors made collectors salivate. The "modern" bronze light fixtures that had replaced the original gaslights sometime in the 1920s had become antiques themselves.

Julia stopped before one of the dark, heavy doors. Hefting a five-inch skeleton key, she fit the complicated head of it into the keyhole. And jiggled and fiddled with it the way she suspected people had jiggled and fiddled with it for the last hundred and forty years. Though they may not have cursed the locksmith in quite as creative

terms as she did. Antique and still unpickable—that
was what they told her every time she complained.
Forget about unpickable; the damned thing was almost
impossible to open when you *did* have a key.

Too bad the conservators weren't still there to let her
in. If it hadn't been for the telecon from hell, she'd have
gotten down to the lab earlier. Instead, she stood
juggling the amulet box and folder of photos while she
fought with the lock. Then again, Paul Wingate and his
staff of conservators were known for keeping eccentric
hours. There was no guarantee they'd have been around.
Temperamental? Sure. Eccentric? Yep. Skilled? Beyond
all doubt. And when you were dealing with history,
skilled won the day.

With a snick the lock turned. "Thank God," Julia
muttered and swung the ponderous door open into
blackness. She'd extended a hand for the switch when
she heard a faint metallic sound behind her. A quick
glance at the deserted hall, gleaming with a soft gray
luster, showed no one in sight. The hairs prickled on the
back of her neck. Probably an echo from the stairwell
around the corner, she told herself firmly. The hard
marble walls magnified sounds, made them travel
farther than they normally would. Security, she decided,
flipping on the lights. Probably doing their rounds.

Fluorescent bulbs flickered to life, gleaming anachro-
nistically in a workshop that was a blend of nineteenth-,
twentieth- and twenty-first-century technologies. Heavy
wooden tables, smoothed from years of use, sat side by
side with white-metal-and-Plexiglas fume hoods more
suitable for a chemistry lab. On one table, someone was
laboriously reconstructing a terra-cotta statue of three
stone figures sitting side by side. By the door, a stone sarcophagus lay on blocks, underneath the railed gantry that

they'd used to hoist it; the actual mummy lay draped on a wheeled table nearby. A tank held some pottery recently acquired from a dig outside of Luxor, soaking in a bath of deionized water.

Nearby lay a section of an Egyptian bas-relief from the museum's permanent collection. Flaking pigment, Julia saw. Setting down the wooden box and the folder absently, she walked forward to study the work. The conservation staff appeared to be laboriously reattaching the flaking pieces fragment by fragment.

Five minutes of it would have had Julia's eyes crossing. The conservators, she decided, deserved to be as eccentric as they liked. After all, it wasn't everyone who could—

She jolted, whipping her head around to stare at the door. A sound. She'd heard a definite, distinct sound that wasn't just her imagination and wasn't just far away. It was here, right outside, coming down the hall. Not a snick of metal, this time, but the quiet pad of footsteps.

Footsteps where no one should be. It wasn't a guard—they jingled and clanked from a mile away. This was someone else, walking down a basement hallway in a museum, an hour after closing, at a time everyone should have been long since gone.

The hairs rose on the back of her neck. The Zander heist had been carried out by a master thief. And if her nervous visitors actually had somehow gotten the White Star from the thief and passed it along to the museum, well, that thief might just be looking for it.

And that thief might just be here.

Quietly, Julia slipped out of her heels and closed her hand around one of the heavy lead weights that sat on the table next to the bas-relief. Holding her breath, she stole forward.

Out in the hall, the footsteps halted before the door.

For a moment, everything was so silent she could hear the pulse thudding in her ears. Then with a creak the doorknob shifted.

Her heart jumped into her mouth. Swiftly, she raised her weapon. The door opened—

And in stepped Alex.

3

Friday, 6:50 p.m.

THE BREATH EXPLODED out of her lungs.

"Jesus, what are you doing down here?" she demanded, knees weak.

He eyed the weight she held. "Clearly, taking my life in my hands."

"It would have served you right if I'd brained you, you idiot. You scared me to death."

"Oh, I don't know," he said, taking the weight out of her hand and setting it on the nearest workbench, "you look pretty lively to me."

She glared at him as he shut the door, willing her system to level, not wanting to admit the relief she felt. Not wanting to admit how good he looked. "How did you find me?" she asked instead.

He shrugged. "I went by your office and saw you walking out of the office wing. I figured I'd follow you."

"No one's supposed to be down here now."

"You're here."

"I'm working."

He made an elaborate show of checking his watch. "Six fifty-four? You didn't tell me you'd switched to swing shift."

"It's your fault." She slipped her shoes back on and walked over to the entrance to the rare-books repository.

"My fault?"

"You brought those people in." The modern door to the climate-controlled room opened with a little hiss of escaping air.

Alex fought a smile. "I take it the flea-market find turned out to be more exciting than you thought?"

"Possibly."

"Where is it?"

Julia turned to point at the wooden box on the table by the bas-relief.

Alex ambled over. "I guess you can get high quality junk in Moroccan bazaars, if you're a choosy shopper." He picked up the box and cracked it open. "Why, I'll bet that—" And then he just stared. "Good Lord," he said slowly.

When his gaze met Julia's, his eyes glowed green with wonder. The quick jolt of connection took her by surprise.

"What is this?" Alex gazed at the amulet, brushing a finger over it.

"Don't touch it," she said, but it sent a shiver through the pit of her stomach. She felt a vibration, as though it were making a sound at some frequency too low to be heard. She swallowed. "I don't know what it is for sure. It could be nothing. It could be an antique forgery. Or it could be a three- or four-thousand-year-old amulet. Take your pick."

He whistled. "Not bad for a flea market. So you came down here to poke around?"

"Exactly. Now, if you'll just give me some privacy…."

"Not a chance." He set the box aside. "Forget about the doodad for a minute. You said last night that we were going to talk, and that's what we're going to do. I think you owe me that, especially after the routine you pulled this morning."

"There's no need for it. Especially after this morning." Julia stepped into the book repository. She just had to remember that it was time to break up with him and get her life in order, not time to fall back into bed with him, despite the little warm flare of arousal that had begun to radiate through her. This was nothing new, it was the same effect he always had on her.

It didn't mean anything.

"I think we got things settled already," she added, busying herself with the computer.

"Oh, I don't think so at all," Alex said easily, pushing the door back to follow her inside. "If you wanted to break up, then what was last night about?"

"Last night was a lapse."

"A lapse? Is that what you call it when you put my—"

"A lapse," she said firmly, struggling to push away the sudden vivid memory of straining naked against him. "It's over with."

"So you've said. I'd just like to be clear on why that is." His voice was reasonable, his expression open.

Julia eyed him warily. She knew this Alex. This was the Alex who almost never walked away from a negotiation without getting what he came for. The Alex whose face said "trust me," even while he was leading his victim down the garden path. This was the Alex who was exceptionally good at getting people to say yes.

People like her.

"We said from the beginning it was going to be casual, that when one of us decided things should be over, they'd be over," she reminded him. That was good. Clear and indisputable.

"I'm just trying to understand."

"I've had some time to think," she said as carefully as though she were picking her way through the jungle, looking for booby traps, watching for the loop that might tighten around her ankle and whip her up to leave her dangling headfirst from a tree. "What I think is that it's best for both of us to end this."

"For us?"

"For me," she amended, flushing.

"And when did you decide that? This morning?"

"I decided it last weekend. I've just been waiting for you to get home."

"Last weekend, huh?" He rested an elbow against the shelves and scrubbed the other through his hair. "But now, here's what I don't get. You let me in last night, right?"

"Yes, but I—"

"And you came to the door in your robe, which didn't stay on very long."

"That's because you—"

"And then you took off my clothes and dragged me down on your living room floor and let me touch your—"

"Skip it."

"All of this after you supposedly decided we were *finito*." His eyes sparkled. "So why was that?"

Because he had a way of making her forget her own name, let alone anything she wanted except him? "It was late, I was tired."

"You seemed pretty frisky to me. Incidentally, did you find a button on your living room floor? Because you ripped one loose when you were taking my shirt off."

"Well, if you'd gotten it off faster, I wouldn't have had to—"

He grinned at her. "Yes?"

Dangling headfirst from a tree. Julia ground her teeth. "I got distracted."

"I don't know, you seemed pretty focused to me. I like those noises you make when you're focused."

Her eyes narrowed. "This isn't a joke."

"I'm not laughing." He reached out to touch the strands of hair that dangled from her chignon.

Julia jerked her head away. "You're not listening either."

"That's because so far nothing you've said has made sense."

Because he'd talked her in circles to where she couldn't remember her points anymore. Her very valid points. Back to basics, she decided. "You're not my type, Alex. And I'm not yours. This was just an…anomaly."

He shifted. "And when I touch your anomaly, some very interesting things happen." He reached out to stroke a finger down her throat.

Julia shivered. "I'm down here to work," she said unsteadily.

"Go right ahead with what you're doing," he told her. "I'll stay out of your way." But his fingertips continued down, into the deep vee at the front of her jacket.

And her muscles weakened. How had he managed to get so close? She could smell a hint of his aftershave, spicy and clean. She could see the gold flecks in the green of his eyes. And she knew what came next, could already feel the tendril of heat curling between her thighs. It was the wrong thing to do, she knew it.

It was nothing she could stop.

"You're not the kind of guy I go for," Julia said, oddly breathless as she leaned into him.

"I can see that," he answered, sliding his hands down over her hips.

"I like serious men."

"I'll buy some glasses."

"This isn't going to change my mind," she warned him, but she'd already slipped her arms around his neck, her fingers up into his hair, because if she didn't have him inside her, soon, she was going to die.

And then he crushed his mouth into hers.

It shouldn't have overwhelmed her. For over six months, they'd been sleeping together. Kissing him wasn't new. She should have been accustomed to it. It shouldn't have started butterflies whirling in her stomach. It shouldn't have made her react.

But she caught her breath and shivered at the taste of him.

And he was smiling, dammit, she could feel his lips curve against hers. He pressed her back against the shelves. "I always have had this librarian fantasy," he murmured, nipping at her lips, dropping his hands down to unfasten the top buttons of her suit jacket. "Papyrus always gets me hot." Then he filled his hands with her lace-covered breasts.

She couldn't stop the moan.

She felt the shelves digging into her back, she knew they had no business doing this here, doing it at all. But his body was so hot against hers that she didn't care. He was hard, she could feel it through his trousers and she twisted against him, wanting more contact, more friction, wanting to dispense with the infuriating barrier of clothing.

With an expert flick he unsnapped the front clasp of her bra, and slipped his hand up over her breast.

The heat, the quick friction was shockingly intimate in the midst of their surroundings. So forbidden. So arousing. Just the night before she'd lain naked against him and yet somehow here in this staid and sedate place, every touch felt like the first. The air was cool against her skin but his hand was hot, so hot. The raw silk of her jacket rubbed against one nipple; his fingers sent bolts of arousal from the other with every brush and squeeze.

It made her feel wild, wanton. It made her ravenous for more.

"God, you drive me crazy," Alex breathed against her neck, inhaling her scent. What would she do if he told her just how much it turned him on that he could make her lose that calm composure of hers? That with mouth and hands he could turn her wild in his arms despite herself. He'd never guessed back before they'd gotten involved just how much heat was there, how much excitement. He'd never thought that she'd make him dry-mouthed with wanting. Now, just the taste of her throat, the feel of her pulse under his lips had his cock straining for release.

He felt her shiver, felt the rise of goose bumps as he worked his way lower, tasting the hollow at the base of her throat, the fragile skin on the tops of her breasts. Then he went lower still, desire rushing through him as he took her nipple into his mouth, heard her strangled gasp for air as he swirled his tongue around and over the hard little bud, feeling it furl and tighten.

Julia leaned back against the heavy wood shelves feeling only the slick heat of Alex's mouth, his tongue on one breast, his hand tormenting the other. And oh, he knew what she liked, the rough scrape of teeth amid the slick caresses.

And the tightness, the growing tightness between her thighs where she knew she was growing wet, where she could feel the pulse of blood thudding.

"So just what do you have on under this?" he murmured, sliding his palms down her hips and up under her narrow skirt, using both hands to slide the fabric up, trailing along the silky hosiery beneath until he hit the tops of the thigh-highs she'd begun wearing habitually since they'd been involved. "Oh, *honey*," he said explosively.

And then his fingers journeyed higher, slipping under the edge of the silk and lace she wore. He stroked her with a touch that shot through her like fire.

And oh, his hands were persuasive, fingers moving, circling, teasing her clit. She couldn't get her breath. She clutched him against her because the heat and the pressure and the friction were tightening and tightening and carrying her along in a mad rush of sensation. She burst into orgasm, shaking against him, gripping him as the only solid thing in the universe.

It left her weak and gasping, half dizzy with reaction. With all that they'd done in the past, it had never been as intense as this. But it wasn't enough, because he was still kissing her, and to her shock, need built afresh even as the orgasm receded.

Sudden compulsion flowed through her. She had to touch him. She fumbled for his zipper and he groaned as she brought him out, hard and heavy. They might not know each other at all but she knew how he liked it. She knew how to make him shudder and jolt. She knew how to take him so close to the edge, push him so far that he was grinding his teeth to maintain control.

Sinking to her knees, Julia breathed on the swollen head of his erection. She teased it with the tip of her tongue, licking first one side, then the other, quickly, experimentally. And then she slid his cock into her mouth in one quick rush, taking it as deep as she could, ripping a helpless moan from his throat.

It intoxicated her, as it always did. It aroused her.

Maybe she was a little out of her depth with Alex, but when she was tasting him, feeling him hard against her lips, feeling his body quake with her every movement of her tongue, she was the one in control. She could play him, speeding up the motion, slowing it down. She could stroke him with hand and mouth and do everything she could to bring him to the edge because she knew he wouldn't want to come that way. She wanted to tease him. She wanted to push his self-control to the limit until he had to beg her to stop.

And she smiled when she felt his hands on her shoulders, dragging her up.

"Let's go down here to the reference desk," Alex said huskily, leading her through the stacks to the row of reading tables against the wall.

"You know, when I was in high school, I had this thing for our librarian." He walked Julia back until she felt the seat of one of the wheeled chairs against the backs of her knees. "She was fresh out of school, so she used to wear her hair up like yours and these tidy little suits, I guess to make herself look older. I used to fantasize about her, about what she had on underneath. Maybe I should check that out before you check out my books, Miss Covington." He slid Julia's skirt up and pressed her into the chair.

Shrugging off his jacket, he knelt before her. Strong and warm, his hands parted her thighs. His eyes were hypnotic. She was dissolving she was so wet, so ready for him to touch her.

"Look at you, so prim in your suit, with all these books around," he breathed, leaning in to lick her thigh above the stocking, sliding his hands up over her breasts. His breath was warm as a touch, sending little shivers through her, all of it focused on that spot where she ached for him. "Oh, yeah, you're better than any fantasy."

He draped her legs over his shoulders, then hooked the scrap of silk out of his way. Helplessly Julia let her head drop back. She felt him trace one finger, then the tip of his tongue through those soft, private folds, making her shudder. And then the time for teasing was done and he found her with his mouth in a slick caress that had her crying out and arching against him.

If he'd tantalized before, now he was relentless, driving her up, eyes hot and intent. He didn't keep to a rhythm but changed his speed and touch continuously until she could only quake and gasp, waiting for the next touch, waiting for the next taste that would send her over.

She heard a high-pitched gasping and she realized that it was her, and her world focused down to the heat of his mouth, the torment of his hands on her breasts and the want, the want, the want that dragged her closer, always closer as every muscle in her body tightened into the ultimate arousal. So close, teetering on the edge.

When he pulled away, she cried out, until she realized that he'd dragged out his wallet to get at his emergency condom, sheathing himself and thrusting into her with a slick, hot rush that had her crying out again. Then he was moving in her, hot and hard and relentless, using the chair to slide her on and off his cock, teasing her with little strokes and then thrusting himself home hard. And giving her that sweet, good friction that took her up and made everything he'd done with his mouth seem inconsequential next to this hard, insistent reality that dragged her up and up until she was balanced on the edge. And then with another stroke she went over, so that she was falling, shuddering and clenching around him. It was that, finally, that sent him surging against her for a handful of hard, quick strokes to spill himself even as she still shook.

And then Julia heard the noise through the still open door.

She tensed. "What was that?"

"What?" Alex asked hoarsely.

"That noise. Outside." She scrambled away. Heart hammering, she dragged down her skirt, buttoning her jacket and fighting a growing sense of embarrassment and horror.

Someone was there, and heaven only knew who. What if they'd heard? What if they'd seen? What if she and Alex were busted? Catching her breath, expecting the worst, she hurried out the open door into the main conservation lab.

Only to find it empty. No one there, she saw with a rush of gratitude. No guards, no conservators, no staffers wondering what was going on in the stacks. Just a quiet, empty conservation lab. They hadn't gotten caught, despite taking an absurd chance. Relief flooded through her.

And then she saw.

"*Alex.* The box."

"The box?"

"The amulet," she almost wailed. "Oh, my God. Did you move it?"

"I put it right back where it was. Right there." He pointed to the table with the bas-relief, but where the open box had been now sat...

Nothing.

Anxiety swept through her. She couldn't stop staring, blinking as though the box would magically appear.

But it didn't. No box, no amulet, just the folder of photographs and drawings, with the smooth table behind it.

The White Star was gone.

4

ALEX STARED AS JULIA rushed over to the door.

"What are you doing?"

"Someone took it," she said, practically vibrating with tension. "It was here and they took it. It wasn't an accident, they had to know what it was. We've got to catch them." She clutched at the knob.

"And what then? Say, 'Give it back pretty please'? No way. We call the guards." Alex spun around to grab the nearest phone.

Only to hear silence. "It's dead," he said just as she said, "It's locked."

"What do you mean?" They spoke at the same time, stopped at the same time.

And stared.

Alex answered first. "The phone line's dead. Did you hear anything about them taking the phones down this weekend?"

"I don't recall, but we've got a bigger problem than that." Julia twisted the black knob in her hand. "The door won't open."

"Try it again. It's an old door. It's probably stuck."

"It's not stuck."

Impatiently, he strode over to give it a careless tug.

He was surprised to feel it solidly unmoving. His eyes narrowed and he took a better grip and pulled.

It made no difference. Okay, not humorous. Alex twisted the handle, listening. "The knob's moving. Maybe something's out of whack with the linkage."

Julia shook her head. "There shouldn't be. They take good care of it. It's hard to get the key in the right spot, but once you do, it turns smooth as—" She broke off.

"What?" Alex asked, but she was already leaning in to stare at the lock.

"I always leave the key in the lock when I come down here because it's so hard to get it in the right spot on the tumblers." She put her eye to the keyhole. "And it's still there."

"So what's the big deal?"

She didn't answer and he saw the familiar air of abstraction on her face. She could say all she wanted to that he didn't know her, but he could see when her mind was vaulting along one of its lightning chains of thought.

She just wasn't always good about clueing anyone else in.

He watched her cross to the tool bench and search its surface. "What's going on in that head of yours, Julia? Help me out here."

"I just want to check and see if…aha!" She held up a piece of thin wire triumphantly. "Here." She came back over and threaded the wire between the door and jamb, then slid it up and back down along the edge of the wood. "The crack's too narrow to see into but—" The motion of the wire stopped. "See? Something's blocking the wire. It's the bolt, thrown over. This door is locked."

"So we unlock it." It seemed simple enough, until

he realized there was no thumbscrew below the knob for unlocking it from the inside. "What kind of damn fool locksmith doesn't put a manual latch on the inside?" he growled.

"One who wanted things to be really safe."

"Well, I'm feeling a little too safe. Let's figure out how to unlock it."

"I'm not sure it's that easy," she said slowly. "The key's still in it."

He felt the first flickers of frustration. "So? It's an antique. How hard can it be? We get some tools and we pick it."

"You can't pick it. The key's in the way. You can't reach the tumblers."

Alex reached for her wire. "Then we push the key out."

"You can't," she said faintly. "Once it's locked, you've got to turn the key back a full revolution to get it out of the keyhole. The end of the key has these flanges...."

He eyed Julia. "You're not being very helpful."

"It's an incredibly complex but an incredibly good lock. That's why they left it in place during all the renovations. There's a line of safes over in the UK that are based on this design."

"Well, we've got to figure out a way to get out."

"That's what I'm trying to tell you. We're not going to get out through that door without help." She swallowed. "We're locked in."

ALLARD WALKED DOWN the street in the gathering twilight, sleek and satisfied as a cat with a dish of cream. She was his again, *his*. The days and nights of frustration meant nothing. Now he had only to slide his hand into his pocket to feel her, warm and smooth against his fingers.

It had been laughably easy to stay in the museum undetected, to watch, to wait. He'd expected to break into the woman's office once night had fallen and the guards retired to their control room. Who'd have guessed she would make it so easy for him, walking out of her office with a box that so obviously held something precious?

Instinct had told him to follow. And there, his impatience had nearly betrayed him, when he'd almost found himself stumbled upon by the lovesick fool on her heels. *Idiot,* he could hear his father's sneer. *Amateur.* Only quick reactions had let Jean whisk out of sight in the stairwell to pursue the woman's pursuer.

Ultimately, it had been to his advantage, for he'd seen the cameras as the young fool had opened the door to the basement. Of course, a clever man carried a small, telescoping steel rod for just such occasions, a rod that could nudge a camera a crucial fraction of an inch, enough to leave a small area unmonitored without making a change large enough to alert the guards.

Once he'd done that, it had been easy to move down the hall undetected, to find them. Of course, taking the amulet had been almost no challenge at all with the two so absorbed in one another. Bah. Only a weak man lost sight of the world because of a woman. And weak men made mistakes—mistakes that could help him.

He'd listened as their discussion had quieted, crept into the outer room as they'd touched one another among the books. And he'd watched a moment, as any man would, savoring the gleam of the woman's bare breasts and feeling his body tighten as she moaned.

But he had not come there for pleasure. He'd come for the amulet, and when he'd opened the box to see the glowing ivory of the White Star, he'd nearly shouted aloud in triumph. He hadn't, though. Instead, he'd tucked the box into his jacket and stolen to the door, turning the key behind him. He'd already taken a moment to provide them with a few…challenges.

And now, he was on the street in the growing darkness, the place he had always felt most strong. And he was strong. He'd recovered his prize. She would bring him pleasure, she would bring him respect.

And she would bring him rewards beyond measure.

JULIA'S FISTS ACHED from hammering the heavy oak door. Tired and hoarse from yelling, she tucked her little fingers in her mouth and blasted a shrill whistle.

Alex paused in what he was doing to give her a startled glance. "Where'd you learn that?"

"Summer camp."

"Not just another nice society girl," he observed.

She hammered at the door again, cursing a blue streak. Alex raised his eyebrows. "Definitely not another nice society girl."

"I can't believe no one's coming."

"It's Friday night," he said mildly. "Everyone's long gone."

"Did you try the other phones?" she asked.

"Dead," he said.

"How can every single phone in the place be out?" she fumed, picking up a receiver only to slam it down.

He snapped his fingers. "Not every phone," he said, spinning toward the book repository.

"Wait." Julia scampered after him.

Alex snatched his jacket from the floor. "I am such an idiot. I don't know why I didn't think of this before." Digging into the breast pocket, he pulled out a slim silver cell phone. "Ladies and gentlemen—" he flourished it "—we bring you rescue, courtesy of your local wireless network."

"That's not your regular phone."

"I upgraded," he said with relish. "I've got half of my CD collection loaded in this baby, plus it's got a high-res camera and it's Web-enabled."

She gave him the same look his mother had given him in fourth grade when he'd listed the many attributes of a new Transformer he absolutely required. "Does it tie your shoes for you, also?"

"When I need it to." A succession of images flowed across the screen as it booted up. "But the best part is that it gives me serious connectivity." He punched up the number and held the phone to his ear.

"For a mover and shaker like yourself, a must."

"Hey, you never know when Blaine Trump will be calling to donate a few hundred grand." His brows drew together as he studied the screen.

"What?"

He walked out into the main lab, holding the phone in front of him and watching the display. "Just trying to get a signal."

"Tell me you're joking."

"Don't worry, we'll get it," he said, trying different areas of the room.

"And security's going to be by any minute."

"They might," he said reasonably. "Sometimes the signal comes and goes."

"And right now it's mostly going, right?"

They stared at each other.

"Maybe in a little while," he said, setting it down on one of the tables.

"Don't set that down and forget where you put it,"

Julia said. "We might need it later. Why don't you have a belt clip?"

He sent her a revolted look. "You're joking, right? Only tech-support dweebs at Computers R Us wear belt clips."

"Which you are not."

"Which I, most definitely, am not. My phone'll be just fine here," he said, setting it on the table. And then he stared beyond it. "What is that?" he asked warily.

"Where?"

"There. On the table." He pointed to a long form lying on a wheeled table behind the sarcophagus and shrouded in translucent plastic.

Enjoyment glimmered in her eyes. "That's Felix."

"Felix?"

"Our new mummy."

Alex pressed his lips together and walked over closer to it. "A mummy. You mean like a four-thousand-year-old dead-guy mummy?"

"Thirty-five hundred in this case, we think, but yes. We just got him in a few days ago."

"Can I look at him?"

"You might not want to," she cautioned, but he'd already pulled up the plastic.

"Jesus. You didn't tell me he was unwrapped."

"Only partially. Felix has had some challenging times."

"So I smell." It was faint but distinct. Now that he'd lifted the plastic, there was the sweet scent of decay. Still, curiosity overcame his initial surprise, prompting him to raise the sheet again. "Dressed for casual Friday, huh, Felix?" He dropped the sheet back down and focused on the problem at hand. "Okay. So let's see…locked door, no windows, no phones, no one coming when we call, and a thirty-five-hundred-year-old mummy. This is beginning to get entertaining."

"I'm glad you're enjoying yourself." Julia tucked the plastic back in place. "Personally, I've got plans for this weekend. I can't stay here."

"Not even to keep Felix company?"

"No."

"Not even to keep me company?" He stepped up behind her to rest his hands on her hips, those deliciously slender, surprisingly flexible hips, and leaned in to nibble on her earlobe.

"Alex." She twisted away. "This is serious."

His mouth curved. "Don't worry about it," he said easily. "The only place people get locked in for days is the movies. Security will be by in a while to let us out."

"Let's hope it's soon."

"Anyway, there's got to be another way out of here." He began to prowl the room. "No extra doors in the book room, right?"

"Right."

"What's this room in here?" he asked, opening the door next to the repository.

"The scientific lab."

He reached inside to flip on the lights and blinked. "Christ. What are all these gadgets?" The room was as modern as the rest of the lab was retro, with shining white walls and gleaming chrome-and-black equipment.

"Oh, a scanning electron microscope, a laser, a Fourier—"

"Okay, I get it." He scanned the room and ducked back out. "If we're bored later, you can teach me how to use them."

"We're not going to be here later, remember?"

"Exactly."

The main conservation lab was in the shape of a thick sideways L balanced on its short leg. To the right of the main door lay the inner wall that formed the library and the scientific lab; combined with the rest of the L, it formed a rectangle maybe fifty feet deep by a hundred feet long.

"What's down here?" Alex asked, skirting the outer wall of the scientific lab to follow the long arm of the L.

"More workspace. The supply room. The chemical shower. The bathroom."

"Thank God for small favors. What's behind this door?" He twisted the knob with no more success than the front door.

"Oh, that's the head conservator's office. Paul Wingate. It's just a nook, though. No way out."

"Let's not rule anything out sight unseen." He studied the modern lock on the door. "That one we might have a chance at."

"For all the good it will do you. And there aren't any ways out of the supply room, either, so I guess that means we're stuck."

"Not for long. I'm telling you, security will find us."

Julia paced across the lab. "What if they don't?"

He couldn't help watching her. "We get out Monday morning when everybody comes to work."

"I can't wait that long. I can't miss this thing tomorrow night."

"What is it?"

"The New York Performing Arts Institute gala. My mother's pet project. She's been working on it for four months and if I'm not there, I'll be hearing about it for at least that long." She moved restlessly across the lab, scanning the walls and ceiling, picking up the phone again, only to shake her head.

"What about a computer?" Alex asked suddenly.

"A computer?"

"Sure. E-mail. The Internet. We ought to be able to

get a message to someone, even just to ask them to call the cops for us." He looked around. "Don't they have one in here?"

"I don't know," Julia said dubiously. "There's a computer in the rare-book repository but it's off-line, just for indices and electronic research."

"Nothing out here?"

She shook her head helplessly. "Too much dust from all the stone. It's not the greatest environment. Most of the staff have cubes upstairs. Paul's the only one with an office down here."

"And his is locked." Alex walked over to the work-bench.

"What are you doing?"

"Looking for some wire."

"And that would be because…?"

"I'm going to try to pick that lock."

"Oh, of course. Got experience at it, do you?"

"I'm a man of many talents."

She watched as he located some stiff wire and used pliers to bend the top quarter inch to a right angle. "Did you apprentice with a second-story man in your youth?"

"Hey, I got my Boy Scout merit badge in B and E."

Julia snorted but watched with interest as Alex nudged his ersatz picks into the lock on Paul's door. "I should object, you know. You're violating the privacy of a staffer."

He flicked her a glance. "Duly noted. I'll lock up again when I'm done, and if you want to stay in here as penance when they come to let me out, feel free." He closed his eyes as he manipulated the tools, completely focused on the hidden workings of the lock.

And somehow, she found herself completely focused on him. This was ridiculous. Quite aside from the fact

that she'd already decided their…arrangement was
history, she had far more important things to worry
about than the length of his lashes and the way his five-
o'clock shadow darkened his jaw.

She made herself look away. "I don't see what
good it'll do you if you get in, anyway. You don't
know his password."

"It might be scribbled down somewhere. It might be
something common. Mine's set to remember so that all
I have to do is hit Enter."

Her mouth dropped open. "You're not supposed to
do that."

He flicked her an amused look. "Uh-oh, are you
going to tell?"

"Alex—"

"Look, it's a long shot, but we might get lucky."

"We'll be lucky to even get through the door."

"When have I not been lucky?" Alex grunted. "Got
it!" Rising, he stuck a hand inside to turn on the light,
swinging the door wide and stepping into the familiar
chaos that was Paul's world.

Alex stared, hands on his hips. "Man, how does he
get any work done in here?" he asked in disgust.

"People who break and enter don't have a whole lot
of room for complaint," Julia pointed out, but she
didn't blame him.

The eight-by-ten office was crammed with books,
papers and tools, cast-off silicone molds of carvings
and a host of other things Julia couldn't identify. The
desk nudged against the far wall was nearly covered
with papers and books. The spare chair merely provided
a resting place for still more. A chemical-stained lab
coat hung from a hook on the door.

Not for the first time Julia wondered how the irascible conservator ever managed to find anything. Brilliant, he might be, but neat was not his strong suit.

"How does he rate a laptop?" Alex demanded in an injured tone. "I begged for six months and they wouldn't give me one."

Julia bit her lip to cover a smile. "He travels to a lot of conservation conferences."

"I travel."

She drew up the extra chair. "I guess he's cuter than you are."

"Hard to believe," Alex muttered dusting the computer off. He reached beyond it to pick up a coffee mug stuffed with metal rods. "What is this stuff?"

"Oh, scalpels, dental tools, glass stirrers…" Julia reached over to pull out a hollow brown rod that looked like a paintbrush without the brush. "And African porcupine quills."

"African porc—" Alex gave her a suspicious look. "You're joking."

"Nope," she said serenely. "They make great probing tools."

"And the bags of dirt?"

"Excavation dirt. We save everything. You never know when you might need it."

"You're all nuts," he muttered, staring at a jumble of small stone and plaster blocks at the back of the desk. He stacked some books on one of the piles and reached for the laptop.

"Oh, don't put those there." Adroitly, Julia shifted the books away from the wooden box Alex had set them on. "That's an artifact box."

"And it'll protect whatever's inside. Isn't that the point?"

"The last thing we need is for it to fall over or something." Julia glanced more closely at the box and made a noise of annoyance.

"What's wrong?" Alex asked.

She blew out a breath. "Paul. He's got this little problem with following procedure. This is still supposed to be in inventory storage. It's still got the pull slip on it." Julia cracked open the top to reveal a stone figure of Anubis, the jackal-headed Egyptian god of the dead.

"Maybe he's trying to clean or do conservation stuff or whatever."

"He still should have done his paperwork. He didn't even notify me."

"'Your rules mean nothing to me'?"

"More like 'My work is too important for me to worry about your stupid bureaucracy.'"

"Sounds like a charmer. So why don't you lay down the law to him?"

Julia sighed. "It's not my place. He doesn't report to me. And, anyway, he's really, really talented. Last summer, we cleaned up our inventory. We get lots of bits and pieces of things in here from digs, stuff that we don't know where it belongs. Paul found the nose of Xerxes."

Alex's mouth twitched. "The nose of Xerxes?"

"A marble bust we've had for forty years. For forty years, it's been missing its nose and Paul recognized it at a glance. He's got this amazing sense for the shape and form of things. When someone's that good, you cut them a lot of slack."

"So he's sloppy. Nobody's good at everything," he observed. "Except me, of course."

"Except you," she said drily. "Although you might wait to congratulate yourself until you've gotten the job done."

He gave her a look that shivered into her bones. "I always get the job done, darlin'," he drawled.

"Big talk."

"It's not just talk. You of all people should know that. Anyway, sloppy isn't always a bad thing," he said cheerfully. "Our boy slapped his computer shut a little too quickly, before it finished closing down."

"So?"

He gestured at the e-mail application on the screen. "So everything's still running. That means we'll still be online."

Despite herself, she was impressed. "That'll help. Good job."

"Feel free to shower me with all the affection you like," he invited.

Julia rolled her eyes. "Just send the e-mail, will you? We've got to get out of here and notify someone that the amulet is gone."

"Long gone, at this point. It's not like the cops are going to find them."

"I hope they do. That amulet might be the White Star, stolen from Zoey Zander's collection."

"The Stanhope heist?"

"Yes."

Alex's fingers flew over the keys. "What is it, Egyptian?"

"I don't think so. A neighboring kingdom. There's some sort of a superstition about it, that it brings good luck to the pure of heart."

Alex made a noise of irritation at the computer. "It didn't bring good luck to us."

"You're hardly pure of heart."

"But I'm pure in other places." He frowned and tapped some more keys. "So what happens with Marissa?"

"Don't remind me," Julia groaned and dropped her head into her hands. "How am I going to tell her? She brings the amulet here to me, I tell her I'll take care of it and it winds up stolen. It's going to reflect terribly on the museum. And me."

"Yeah, well, we've got a bigger problem than that," he said grimly.

"What do you mean?"

He pointed to the screen. "The network's down."

5

"WHAT?" Julia stared at Alex.

"The network's down. Look."

Network not available. The black letters on the screen seemed to vibrate, taunting her. "How can it be down?" she demanded. "I don't believe this. No phones, no cell phone, no Internet. What the hell's going *on?*" Unable to sit still, she jumped up and began to pace. "What are we supposed to do?"

Alex considered. "We could have sex."

"Will you be serious for once?" she snapped. "This is all your fault."

His mouth dropped open. "What did I have to do with it?"

"If it wasn't for having sex, we wouldn't be locked up here in the first place." She strode out of the lab. "If you'd just listened to what I said this morning. But no, you had to come down here and distract me and then start fooling around—"

"Oh, I don't know, I sort of got the impression you liked the fooling around. Or were those hummy noises you made a signal to go away?"

She flushed. "That's not the point."

"That's exactly the point," he countered. "I wasn't in

there alone and you weren't exactly saying no. Who was it who unzipped my pants?"

It mortified her that he was right, mortified her that she had zero self-control where he was concerned. "Fine. So I got into it."

"Hell yeah, you got into it and so did I. Why is that such a bad thing? Why don't you just admit that you want me as much as I want you?"

"I don't *want* to want you," she almost wailed. "Look at what's happened here. It's a perfect example of why you don't belong in my life."

"Why, because someone got in here while we were busy and walked off with the goods? You know what they've said about the Stanhope job. It was pulled by a professional. You don't think a pro would have found a way to get the amulet anyway?" He took a step closer to her. "More to the point, would you really have wanted to be down here alone when he came looking?"

It stopped her for a moment, but then she recovered. "What makes you so sure it was a he?"

"He, she, doesn't matter. You saw *Kill Bill*, didn't you?"

"I sincerely doubt the amulet was stolen by a sword-wielding assassin in a yellow tracksuit."

"True, yellow is too garish. But you have to admit, another color is a possibility."

"Will you be serious for once?" And then she stared at him, suddenly appalled. "You don't think he watched us, do you?"

Alex's mouth twitched. "I don't think tracksuited assassins are into that sort of thing."

"I never *did* that sort of thing before I met you." She began pacing again.

"You never had sex?" He shook his head pityingly. "Think of all the years you squandered."

"I mean I never let myself get finagled into having sex in public places where people could watch."

"You call this public? After the hotel balcony and the jazz cruise and the taxicab? This is practically private."

"Except for our friend."

"Forget about him. Let's go back to the finagling part."

"Easy for you to say. You weren't the one who had your top unbuttoned."

"That's right, you did," he said softly, sliding his fingers down the nape of her neck.

"Stop that." She batted his hands away. "That's how this whole thing got started. All we need is for the security guards to come in and find us next." Abruptly she let out a despairing sigh. "If they ever do."

"WAKE UP, HARRY."

The stocky, gray-haired security guard sitting before the bank of television monitors jumped. "Jeez, Fletcher, you putz, you scared the hell outta me."

"Nice to have you awake."

"Funny guy. You're a funny guy," Harry muttered bad temperedly as Fletcher crossed the monitor room to flop down in one of the dilapidated chairs.

"So, you been doing anything besides feeding your face while I been out patrolling?" Fletcher asked, picking up Harry's empty can of barbecue Pringles.

"Hey, it ain't easy to watch eight monitors at once. It takes skill, which is why you're not qualified. Just walk the floors until we get you trained and everything'll be fine. Unless you want to go back to day shift."

"Hell no. Longest eight hours around, standing in one of those galleries watching people walk through. It's enough to get you half-nutty, you know what I mean? You start making up stories about people."

"I don't think that's the job, Fletcher, I think you were half-nutty to begin with."

"Ha-ha. Like you're not, sitting here all night staring at TVs that don't change. Or are you focused on the one that does?" he asked, pointing at the portable television Harry had set up.

"Hey, it's the Yanks against the Mets. No way I'm gonna miss a chance to see Pedro kick Yankee butt."

"And of course you ain't gonna miss anything on the other TVs while Jeter's hitting a long ball off him."

Harry glowered. "You do your job, Fletcher, and I'll do mine."

"I got a better idea. You do the patrolling and I'll watch the game. I been through those upper floors and the parking lot until I'm seeing things."

"Don't be such a crybaby. All you got is two floors. You don't gotta do the top and you don't gotta do the basement, am I right? That's because of this little screen here and this little screen here that watch all the doors and the elevator. That's me, huh? Me doing all the work so you can put your feet up."

Fletcher glowered at him. "You're a regular prince, Harry. You are. Now you got any more Pringles or don't ya?"

JULIA PACED AROUND THE LAB. "Okay, we've tried the phones, we've tried the computer, we've tried the doors. Nothing doing. Any other ideas?"

Alex glanced up from rolling up his sleeves. "We could yell some more." He folded up the tie he'd removed and set it aside.

"Not helpful. Come on, we're intelligent, resourceful people. We've got all the tools we could possibly use."

"Hey, I already told you one guaranteed way out. We

just need to put a flame up by one of the sprinklers. It'll start the alarms."

"And the sprinklers. Water everywhere. You want to take responsibility for destroying a twelfth-dynasty sarcophagus, an eighteenth-dynasty mummy and an early-period bas-relief? Because I sure don't."

"You don't know, Felix might like it. Bet he hasn't had a shower in a couple thousand years."

"Can you please be serious?"

"Not willingly." And then he slapped himself on the forehead. "Duh." Hopping to his feet, he crossed to the workbench.

"What are you doing?"

"Looking for a hammer and screwdriver. This is so obvious I don't know why I didn't think of it before. The hinges are on our side, right? All we have to do is knock out the hinge pins and we can pull the door out backward." He shoved a pair of pliers in his back pocket.

"What are you, nuts? You'll wreck the hinges."

"I'm not going to wreck the hinges. And so what if I do scratch them up a little?"

"They're *antiques*. The bolt on this door is about two inches long. You try to pull it out and you're going to mess up the jamb, at the very least, if not the door and the lock."

He gave her a mulish look. "Look, do you want out or not?"

"I don't want out that badly. My job is to preserve things, not to wreck them. If the place was on fire, yeah. In this case, no way."

"And she says she wants out." Alex gazed up at the ceiling, as though he might find patience there. And then he froze. "Oh, wait," he said slowly. "We are so out of here."

"Not the door," she warned him.

"Not the door."

"So, what, have you figured out a way to walk through walls?"

"Don't have to," he said. "We're going over them."

"YOU'RE OUT OF YOUR MIND," Julia said as she balanced on the corner of one of the sturdy wooden tables in her stocking feet.

"I know exactly what I'm doing. An acoustical ceiling is a bunch of tiles suspended in a metal grid that hangs from the subflooring of the level above on wires. You push up the tiles, there's open space. You can climb over the wall from here to the corridor."

"Alex, there's a wall there. We're not going to be able to crawl over."

"First, only one of us needs to crawl over. Second, this is a side hallway, not a main corridor. It's highly unlikely it's a load-bearing wall. In that case, there's a good chance there are only studs above the door, no lath and plaster. They'd only have built as high as the ceiling."

"You are aware that they didn't have acoustical ceilings back in the 1870s, right? The original ceiling's probably up there somewhere."

"I doubt it." He moved next to the table. "Why go to the trouble of putting in a second ceiling in a workshop? It's not like it needs to look pretty. It'd cost money, take time, close down the lab."

"Then why did they put it in, genius?"

He shrugged. "There was probably a burst pipe at some point and they had to replace the ceiling. What's easier, encasing the pipes in more plaster or putting up a nice acoustic ceiling that will let you at 'em any time you have trouble in the future? Why do you think there are acoustical ceilings in the halls down here?"

"All right, maybe you have a point," she said reluctantly.

"Maybe. That's why we're going to take a look. If there's any room between the acoustical tile and the subflooring for the floor above, we should be able to cross over from this side to the corridor side and get out."

She crossed her arms and stared down at him. "So if 'we' are going to be able to do that, then why am *I* the one who's got to sit on your shoulders and check it out?"

"Because I don't think you want me on your shoulders." His teeth gleamed. "Anyway, it's the only way to get enough height. Those rolling toolboxes aren't strong enough to take my weight and I'm not going to split a gut hauling one of those big wooden tables over here until I know this'll work. Relax. All you have to do is take a little horsey ride over to the door, lift up the acoustic tile, peek and you'll be done."

Peek and you'll be done. Perfect. Someone was going to get a peek. Someone was going to get an eyeful. She couldn't have pulled trousers out of the closet that morning, oh no. And, of course, the museum didn't believe in casual Fridays. Unfortunately, her suit came with a snug miniskirt that didn't exactly lend itself to riding on a man's shoulders.

Julia sighed and put her hands on her thighs, ignoring Alex's puzzled look. With a little shimmy she began to slide the claret silk up her hips, revealing the lace at the top of her stockings and the silky triangle of black fabric above.

He pursed his lips as he looked up at her. "Let me guess, you've really always yearned to be an exotic dancer."

"Cut the wisecracks," she replied, face flaming. "Turn around, will you?"

"Okay," he said, but his eyes darkened, she saw it before he turned to back up to the table. "Mount up, cowgirl."

Steadying herself on his shoulders, Julia slung one leg over one of his shoulders. Almost automatically he curved his hand around her stockinged calf. Heat bloomed up her leg. God, she was pathetic, like Pavlov's dog. She saw him getting turned on and suddenly she was the one getting aroused. This was the man she wanted out of her life, she reminded herself.

She hesitated.

"What's the holdup?"

"I don't have anything to hold on to to get on."

Alex shifted to turn sideways to the table and she yelped.

"Relax, okay? I've got you. I'm not going to let anything happen to you." He slipped his free arm behind the leg she stood on and edged closer to the table, raising his arm up like one of the Egyptian figures on the bas-relief. "Now, press on my hand and just kind of slide your leg onto my shoulder."

His grip was solid, reassuring. It took a couple of tries, but finally she was perched on his shoulders, the ceiling now maybe four or five inches away. And the floor a long way down, she realized, wobbling a little.

"How are you doing up there?"

"I know what it feels like to be a basketball player."

He chuckled and tightened his grip on her legs, which helped in the stability department but did nothing for her state of mind. She tried to ignore the feel of his palms pressed against her calves, his hair brushing against the sensitive skin of her thighs.

And the fact that his neck was pressed firmly between her legs. Only a thin layer of fabric separated the heat of his skin and her most sensitive places. She shifted and felt a sudden, surprising little twinge of arousal at the motion.

Oh no, not this. It was a joke. She was in the most undignified position she'd ever been in, skirt up around her waist, sitting on his shoulders like some groupie at a rock concert. She was mortified, annoyed, embarrassed, uncomfortable.

And yes, turned on.

Ridiculous, Julia thought impatiently. She had a job to do.

She didn't need to get done.

She wasn't going to let herself be led around by her hormones, even if she knew the divine things he could do with that clever mouth of his. Her eyes narrowed. "You planned this, didn't you?"

"Who, me?" Alex's voice was guileless as he started walking the dozen feet to the door. "I'm just trying to get you out so that you can get to your weekend plans, even if they don't include me. I'm hurt that you'd suspect my motives." He kissed the inside of her thigh.

And she felt the arousal again, this time stronger. Then something brushed against her hair. She jerked her head away reflexively and turned quickly to look, except that there was a big difference between moving abruptly when she was on the ground and doing it when she was perched six feet up on a man's shoulders, and suddenly things started to happen way too quickly.

Starting with her yelp.

"What the…?" Alex clamped his hands on her legs. Julia would have applauded the impressive little express soft-shoe he used to try to get beneath her except that she was too busy windmilling her arms to get her balance while she was slipping off his shoulders. In a panic, she gave up and just tried for a handhold, except that the only thing around was Alex's head.

And finally things were steady.

"Can we not do that again?" he asked, his voice muffled. Because her palm and fingers were pressed over his mouth and hooked under his chin, she realized.

With a little cough, Julia released the fingers she'd clamped in his hair. "Sorry. You almost ran me into a sprinkler."

"And that was a real interesting way to tell me about it," he said. "Next time, try just saying 'Sprinkler ho,' or something."

Julia fought a smirk. "Aye, aye, sir."

"Any sprinklers in our path?"

"No, sir. Full speed ahead."

Cautiously, Alex walked to the door, then stopped and stood in front of it. He shifted his head awkwardly to look up. "Okay, can you reach the ceiling tile with some room to spare?"

"I think so."

"There shouldn't be anything holding the panel in place. You should be able to just push and raise it up. They're heavier than you'd expect and sometimes they get a little wedged in place, so be prepared to put some muscle behind it."

"How do you know so much about this, anyway?"

"My uncle's a contractor. I worked summers for him when I was in high school."

Julia put her palms on the tile and pressed up. "Okay, got it."

"What do you see?"

"Black, mostly."

"Here." He handed her a flashlight he'd scavenged.

She aimed the beam into the dark space. "Okay, I see some pipes that look like copper. Water probably, huh?"

"Probably."

"They're not really in the way, but the subflooring of the level above is really low."

"How low?"

"Really low. Like maybe ten inches, if that."

"Enough room to scramble through?"

She looked down at him and sighed. "You'd never make it through in a million years."

"Would you?"

6

JULIA STARED at the patch of missing ceiling over the door and the light that shone through from the hallway, then at the waist-high wooden table that now stood before it. "So let me get this straight. We climb up on the table and you'll boost me up, then I'm supposed to wiggle between the studs and through the gap between the top of the doorjamb and the subflooring above?"

"That's the idea."

"Without breaking the metal stuff that holds up the ceiling tile."

"That would probably be bad," Alex agreed.

"And once I do that, I…what? Swan-dive face-first into the marble floor nine feet below?"

"That would be one approach, I suppose, but it would be a shame to see that pretty face messed up," he said. "See how the ceiling tiles are lined up with their short ends along the wall? I think the best move would be to let me boost you up there legs first and help you get balanced on the top edge of the wall. Then when you're ready, you can move your legs through the hole. I'll help lower you and then all you have to do is jump down, unlock the door and wait for me to open it."

"Julia Covington, human eel," she said drily.

"I'm sure you can do it."

"Your faith is flattering."

"Look at it this way, it'll help your flexibility."

Julia gave him a look under her brows. "I do yoga three times a week. I'm as flexible as I need to be."

"You won't get any argument here," he said.

She moved to step up on a chair to climb on the table and then noticed him out of the corner of her eye, watching her with particular attention. She turned. "What?"

Alex hesitated. "Well, you're not going to want to hear it."

"Hear what?"

"Well, with that skirt and that jacket, you're…"

"I'm what?" She folded her arms.

"Well, that skirt's kind of tight." He looked her up and down. "So's the jacket. Not that I don't applaud the look, but…"

Julia raised her eyebrows.

"It's just that you're going to have a tough time getting through in those clothes," he said in a rush. "You can't move in them and your jacket buttons are going to get caught on things. Plus, you're probably going to wreck the suit."

"Your point?" she asked.

He rubbed the side of his nose. "I think you'd, uh, do better out of them."

"You have got to be kidding." Julia gave him a withering stare. "Are you seriously telling me you want me to strip to try to climb through the ceiling—legs first, by the way—and out into the corridor? Where I'll stand for the fifteen minutes it takes you to shove that monster table out of the way? Oh, hello, Mr. Security Guard, no, nothing's wrong, I just felt like running around the museum naked at night. No, really, I'm not crazy. I work here."

He couldn't entirely hide his smile. "I'm just saying you're going to run into trouble if you try going up there wearing what you're wearing."

She snorted. "I see, it's out of nobility that you're suggesting it. I'll change into a lab coat."

"Still a lot of loose cloth and buttons to catch on things."

"This wouldn't, by any chance, be a way to get me naked, would it?"

He caught her to him. "Darlin'," he growled, "if I want to get you naked, I've got better ways of doing it." He released her just as her brows drew together. "I was *joking*. Look, I just don't want you to get hurt. And if you're not willing to get out of those clothes to try your escape number, then we're better off if you skip it. Maybe I can try."

"There's no way," she told him. "It's going to be a tight fit for me."

"Then maybe we should just wait. What's the worst that happens? So you miss your gig, we cool our heels for a few hours. We'll survive."

She opened her mouth and then closed it again. For a moment, she stood, then she began pacing, making a restless little circle in the center of the lab, looking every so often at the gaps in the ceiling.

Alex simply waited, trying not to be frustrated at the fact that it was she, and not he, who was going to make the attempt. He was the guy, he was supposed to take the risks. Unfortunately, physical realities were physical realities.

And so he watched Julia pace.

Finally she shook her head briskly and walked over. "Nope, not good enough. Let's go do it."

He wasn't prepared for what she did next. He'd expected her to matter-of-factly begin taking off her jacket and skirt. Instead she dropped her hands to her midthigh hemline and began sliding the fabric up, raising her foot to prop it on the chair, pushing the skirt up farther until she'd revealed the lacy top of her stocking. And then she began rolling it down.

There was something about the simple intimacy of the gesture that made his mouth go dry. Mesmerized, he watched her roll the stocking, sliding her hands over her thigh, her calf, tensing her leg. When she pulled the hose off the tip of her toe, he began to hear a faint roaring in his ears. Then she put her foot down and began the process with the other leg, like a woman in her bedroom, undressing for him in a way she never had. Always before, they'd been caught up in the frantic rush of sex, dragging at one another's clothing, tumbling onto the bed or onto or against whatever surface was nearby.

Now, he leaned against the door and just watched as she stepped out of her skirt, as her hands dropped to the buttons of her jacket, freeing them one by one.

He remembered the way they'd slipped through the buttonholes under his fingers earlier. It seemed like an age ago. It felt as if he hadn't had her in weeks, months. Ever. Somehow, in this utterly incongruous environment, it was as though she was revealing herself to him for the first time. And he felt the desire begin to flow, liquid and hot.

When she parted the front of the jacket and slipped it off her shoulders, he felt the punch of it all the way to his toes.

And then she glanced over at him. He saw her breasts rise as she caught a breath.

Heat arced between them.

He didn't think about moving to her; he just did it. He didn't think about pulling her into his arms, but she was there. And when he crushed his mouth against hers, it was hotter than it had ever been with them.

He'd always gotten tired of women quickly. A month, maybe two, and the fascination would wither, their hold on him would weaken. Whereas Julia's only grew stronger. None of the women in his past had matched him wit for wit. None of them had sent arousal drumming in his veins, left him dry-mouthed and desperate with wanting. None of them had made him want the way Julia made him want.

He felt the heat catch with her, felt her shiver under his touch. And then he wasn't in control anymore because suddenly her mouth was avid and greedy against his. With a noise of impatience, she twisted against him to press herself closer, running her fingers up through his hair. And her scent was all around him, her taste permeating him, the way she'd come to permeate his thoughts; his days, his hours divided into time spent with Julia and time spent thinking about Julia.

All he had to do was slide her out of the silk and lace that she wore and he could have her naked. All he had to do was touch her in the ways he knew she couldn't resist and she'd be his, and the need that was pounding in his veins would be assuaged.

But he couldn't.

"Julia," he said quietly.

"What?"

"Stop. Put on your jacket." Gently he pulled away and draped her jacket over her shoulders, trying to ignore the feeling that his belly was filled with sharp rocks. "I think we should stop, okay?"

At first she just blinked at him, half-dazed, and then a deep flush spread over her face. "What kind of game are you playing, Spencer?"

"I'm not playing one."

"Oh, yeah? You could have fooled me."

He shook his head. "No."

"No? You act like you can't keep your hands off me, you make a pass, and then suddenly you're putting on the brakes, when *I'm* saying yes?" Her words vibrated with fury.

"You're not saying yes."

"What's that supposed to mean?"

"That wasn't yes, that was, I don't know, hormones, the moment, call it whatever you want to." He scrubbed a hand through his hair. "I came onto you, you went with it. And it was sexy as hell. But if we go for it, you'll be sorry after. You'll be ticked at yourself and ticked at me and then you'll feel crummy and I'll feel like a creep, and neither of us deserves that. That's not what this is about. That's never what this has been about, and whatever it's missing, feeling good after sex hasn't been it. So let's call a break."

He saw the incredulous look on her face and let out a long breath. "I want you. You know that, and if you have any doubts just look at me and you'll see how much." He gave a rueful glance downward. "But not this way. You change your mind and decide you want this to happen, that's different. You come to me, then I'm there in a heartbeat. But not like this. Okay?"

Julia gazed at him a long moment. He felt ridiculously tense, fighting the urge to hold his breath. Finally, she nodded, almost to herself.

And then she shrugged the jacket aside and climbed onto the table. "Fine. Then get over here and boost me up."

7

"JUST ONE MORE INCH and I'd have made it," Julia grumbled, pacing restlessly around the lab.

"You needed at least two, maybe more."

The wooden table had been moved back into place. She was dressed again, though her hose remained tossed to one side. "I was so close," she groaned.

"You weren't. Hey, how's your leg?"

Not nearly as bumped as her pride, but it was hard to stay angry at Alex. "It's fine. Thanks for finding the first-aid kit."

"I didn't even see that flange when I boosted you up. I'm sorry. I wish it had been me."

It really bothered him, she realized. Not only that he hadn't been able to save the day, but also that she'd gotten hurt trying. "The doctors say the scar will hardly show, dearest," she said in her best Thirties-melodrama voice. "I'll simply add a few ruffles to my costume and it'll be fine. I never had much of a career in shot put anyway."

"No, darling, don't say that," he pleaded, clasping her hands with his. "We'll…we'll get you to that Swiss clinic. A few weeks there and you'll be right as rain."

Julia eyed him. "Swiss clinic, huh?" she asked in a normal voice.

"They're very good, those Swiss."

"I'll keep that in mind. Anyway, we gave it our best shot. That's something, at least."

"Speak for yourself. I'm still working on my best shot." Alex crouched before the door, staring into the keyhole.

"I think you're wasting your time," she said over his shoulder.

He shrugged and worked the wire, trying to reach the tumblers. "What else do I have to do? Besides, I'm feeling frisky after getting into Paul's office." He glanced over his shoulder at Julia. "Of course, if you're feeling frisky, too, I can think of some other options."

Her eyes flashed. "Don't start with that. You were the one who turned me down."

"I turned down your response to my pass," he corrected. "Now, if you want to make a pass on your own recognizance, that's something else entirely."

"No, thanks. I'm feeling of sound mind and body at present."

"I'll vouch for the body part. Hey, ow," he complained as a whiteboard eraser bounced off him. "That was a *compliment*. Now let me concentrate. I'm trying to pick a lock here."

He'd never been able to resist a puzzle, whether it was a lock or a woman whose mouth said one thing while her eyes and body said another. That was Julia, one minute, cool as a cucumber and pushing him away, the next, she'd be pulling him closer. He enjoyed flustering her, enjoyed knowing that no matter how much she didn't want to want him, she still did.

It wasn't enough, though. After six months, he

wanted more. He wanted more of that quick wit and acerbic tongue. He wanted to know more about her complicated mind. He wanted to get into her head and into her life. Unfortunately he'd come to that particular realization at just the time she was trying to walk away.

Slowly, he stopped working fruitlessly to reach the hidden tumblers of the lock. The thief, he realized, had done him a favor. Julia couldn't walk away now, not this time. They were locked in. Together. He had hours, maybe even days, to work on her. Time enough to talk, for a change. Time enough to get to know each other.

Time to win her back.

Which meant that working on the lock was not in his best interest. With an elaborate sigh, Alex rose. "I guess you're right. Doesn't look like I'm going to get anywhere with this." He heard a rumbling noise and flicked a quick glance at Julia. "What was that?" She didn't answer, but he saw her cheeks tint. "Was that you?" he asked.

As though in response, her stomach growled again.

Alex raised an eyebrow. "I guess it's past your dinnertime."

"That's okay. Security's supposed to be here any minute to let us out, isn't that what you said?"

He glanced at his watch. "Eight-thirty. Appears they're running a little late." Casually, he strolled over to one of the workstations and opened a drawer. Notebooks, pens, erasers.

"What are you doing?"

"Just depending on human nature." He searched the open drawer and moved onto the next. Gloves and goggles, some kind of fancy measuring tool.

"Those are people's work areas," Julia said over his shoulder.

"So they are." Giving up on the drawers, he tried opening up the storage unit that hung over the work counter. "Pay dirt," he crowed.

"What did you find?" Julia demanded.

He showed her the candy bar he'd unearthed. "Dinner. Or at least part of it. It seems to me I was supposed to feed you tonight, although I was thinking more Nobu than Snickers."

"At this point, I'll take what I can get," Julia told him. "You know they're not supposed to have anything in here." But she began searching drawers just the same.

Alex laughed. "We already saw how far 'supposed to' goes down here."

"Good point." She pulled open another drawer and stopped. "Whoa. I guess someone works late in the lab a lot." She moved back to let Alex peer over her shoulder at a collection of granola bars, cheese crackers and chocolate drops. When he moved to touch, though, she raised her hand. "Not yet. We should check everywhere first. Find out how much food we've got so that we know whether to ration."

There were times he downright adored her. "You're cute when you get all serious." Alex leaned in to smack her on the lips while her hands were full.

Julia dropped a granola bar. "I'm just being practical," she said, fumbling for it on the floor and bumping her head as she rose.

"I don't know, starvation could stand us in good stead. We get thin enough, we can get out by just slipping under the door." His gaze skimmed her curves. "Of course, you female types have certain, uh, anatomical disadvantages there."

She gave him her countess look again, and he

grinned, and moved on with his search. "How about the refrigerator?"

"Unlikely. That's for chemicals. They know better than to keep food there. At least, they ought to."

"Since when has that stopped anyone?" he asked, walking over to it.

On the front stuck a magnet proclaiming Conservators Do It So It doesn't Show. Inside was a confusion of brown glass bottles and jugs, clear jars sealed in plastic bags. "So what's all this?" Alex gestured at the mix. "I thought they mostly used paint and glue and stuff for restoration."

"We've got quite a bag of tricks these days," Julia said. "That's thioglycolic acid." She pointed at a brown glass bottle. "Good for removing iron stains. And methylcellulose, which is a consolidant."

"Of course it is."

Her lips twitched. "You use it to coat pieces you're going to take a mold of so the silicone doesn't stick and wreck the original."

"But then you've got the problem of methyl whatchamacallit on the original."

"Oh, that comes off with solvent."

"And the solvent comes off with…?"

"Your head." But there was a smile of her lips when she said it, which was progress. "Let's see, what else do we have here… Film, obviously, and *funiori,* which is another consolidant. Japanese. Oh, and isinglass. That's a binder for treating polychrome sculpture. Medieval stuff, mostly, and gilded pieces. I haven't a clue what it's doing here. Paul must be trying something new."

"Paul must be trying something new with this, too," Alex interrupted, reaching past her to pull out a can of

Coke. "What do you think, polychrome sculpture, or stone?" He held it up.

"My stomach," she told him, and took the can.

THEY SAT ON THE WORKBENCH, legs dangling, booty piled at their sides, like kids the day after Halloween.

Alex held up a packet of beef jerky, turning it over in his hands. "You know, this looks an awful lot like old Felix there." He gestured with his chin to the mummy on the far table.

"That's revolting."

"Well, you've got to admit, Felix looks sort of dark and stringy, too." He ripped open the package and pulled out a piece to dangle before her. "Mmm, want some?"

She gave him a pained look. "I'll stick with the candy bars and crackers, thanks."

"Your loss," he said. Taking a bite, he chewed. And chewed and chewed and chewed… Five minutes later, give or take, he swallowed with a gulp. "Okay, maybe I'll pass on the Felix jerky," he muttered. "It's probably cursed anyway." He set the package aside. "What else do we have here?"

"I'll trade you a granola bar for a Twix," Julia offered.

Alex eyed her. "You think I'm going to give up chocolate and caramel for packaged cardboard? My jaws are already tired as it is."

"It's healthier," she wheedled.

He shook his head. "You've got to work on your pitch, sweetheart. First rule of sales, figure out what I want and show me how the deal gives it to me."

"Okay, I'll give you a big, crunchy, tasty granola bar and two luscious Kisses for a measly little Twix."

"Sold!" He reached for her and she gave a startled yelp.

"What are you doing?"

"You said two kisses. Lip only or French?"

"Hershey's," she said drily and held out her hand. "The Twix, please?"

"I'm tastier than candy," he pointed out.

"You're talking about chocolate. It mimics the chemicals released in orgasm, in case you didn't know."

Alex looked at her pityingly. "Do you want a mimic or do you want the real thing?"

"Speaking of pitches…"

"I'm not about to give up because I know you've got a soft spot for me," Alex said, handing her the candy bar and unwrapping one of his own. "What I don't get is why you're so set on this whole breakup thing. We've been having a great time up to now. Why stop?"

"Would you rather be eating granola and chocolate right now or a big, juicy steak?"

"Don't torture me," he said mournfully.

"Exactly. Real food. Alex, the last six months have been a blast, but it was dessert. Junk food, not the real thing. And it was fun and it worked at the time, but it's not enough for me anymore."

"Good. It's not enough for me, either."

"And I'm allergic to peanuts, so I can't eat them," she said, reminding herself more than him.

Alex blinked. "Okay, maybe I should stand up and have you hit me with that one again."

"What I mean is, just because something sounds good doesn't mean that it's good for you."

"Still not following."

How was it that it was so clear in her head and came out so muddled? "Alex, wanting to have a relationship doesn't mean we can do it," she said gently. "I mean, think about it. We don't have anything in common except sex."

"How do you know? We've never really talked about anything."

"Exactly my point. I'm not your type and you're not mine." Oh, but he'd felt like her type, night after night. She frowned at herself. "You like party girls and that's not me. I've just been in a…phase." That sounded reasonable, she thought in satisfaction.

"A phase, huh?"

"Yes."

"Nice phase."

"And done." Her voice was firm.

"So what makes you so sure I'm not your type? Maybe I am and you've never figured it out because you're so sexually insatiable that all you wanted me for was my body." He gave her a wicked look. "I know how you women are, weak vessels of lust."

"Yeah, right, that would be me."

"It's that phase thing." Alex took a drink of his soda. "Okay, so maybe it has been all sex, no talk. Per your request, I might add. Well, we've got time to talk now. Unless you've changed your mind about the sex," he added hopefully.

"You *are* determined."

"You'll break down eventually if we're trapped here long enough." He gave her a slow smile that had her pulse thudding. "You won't be able to resist. But in the meantime, we talk."

"We don't have anything to talk about."

"Sure we do."

"Like what?"

"Anything. Who'd win in a mud wrestling match, Geraldo or Prince Charles? What you think about the possibility of extraterrestrial life. Where you want to be in five years."

She studied him. "You really expect me to take this seriously?"

"Why the hell not? Who else do you have to talk to, Felix?"

The corner of her mouth twitched. "My money's on Geraldo. Prince Charles would get hung up on his dignity thing. He wouldn't get down and dirty."

"Ah, but see, there you go, making assumptions. I think old Chuck might just surprise you. There's no telling what he learned at those English boarding schools."

"I'll keep that in mind." Rising, she walked over to the sink to wash her hands.

"Cleanliness is next to godliness?"

"It is when you're handling rare books. I'm going to research the amulet. That's why I came down here in the first place."

He gave her a puzzled look. "Why bother? It's gone."

"I want to confirm it's the real thing."

"The auction house thought so."

"And auction houses can be fooled. Anyway, what else have I got to do? Besides that," she added firmly as he opened his mouth.

He thought about it a second and stuck his hands under the water. "I suppose."

She watched him. "What are you doing?"

"Trying to be just like you. You're my idol."

"Right. Well, I'm going in here."

"That's okay. Don't worry about me," he called after her. "Me and Felix, we'll just hang."

8

JULIA SETTLED in at the computer in the book repository and inserted a CD-ROM. So she was locked in; she'd probably be down here doing research late anyway. The thing to do was concentrate on the work. Then she wouldn't worry about the locked door, about being cut off from the outside world.

Then she wouldn't worry about Alex.

If only things had worked out as she'd planned. She'd have broken up with him and they'd have gone their separate ways, preferably as quickly as possible. Instead, disaster. Bad enough that she'd wound up blurting it out to him in her office, but then to be locked up together, unable to escape? And he was being great about it, but that really only made it harder.

She knew she wanted it over. It wasn't a snap decision, it was a conclusion she'd reached after giving it serious thought. After all, with the exception of the previous six months, that was how she did everything. Even her marriage had dragged on long after it should have, precisely because she'd wanted to be sure.

When Julia's mind was made up, it was made up.

So Alex was being charming—that didn't erase the reasons she had for wanting to break up with him. She was ready for a real relationship, which meant that Alex, however fun a companion he was, had to go.

The door from the lab opened, and the man in question walked in.

"Bored?" she asked.

"Felix isn't that hot of a conversationalist. Besides, you've heard one tale of the mummy, you've heard them all." He stuck his hands in his pockets. "I figured I could help."

"It probably won't be very interesting," she warned him. "I'm trying to track the amulet back through time. That means going through a lot of dry, old sources to see if there's anything that'll let us conclusively identify it."

Alex looked around the stacks. "You really think you're going to have what you need in here? I did a senior paper on consolidation in the later Roman empire, had to write all kinds of libraries to get translations of original source materials."

Julia blinked. "You did a paper on the later Roman empire?" When she heard herself, she flushed. "I mean…"

"I got a history degree," he said mildly. Studying her obvious surprise, he raised an eyebrow. "You're making assumptions again, Julia."

It stung, all the more so because she deserved the rebuke. "I'm sorry. I just thought…don't you have a business degree?"

"That too. Business degree, MBA, history."

"I didn't realize you'd done so much."

"Ask next time. You'll find out all kinds of things."

"Well, then, you know what we're up against," she said briskly, willing the embarrassment to fade. "But we can still make some progress. The repository isn't intended as an exhibit. It's supposed to be a curatorial resource. We've got some original manuscripts and papyri and books, but we've also got lots of reprints and translations and overviews. Oh, and microfilm and CD-ROMs of the *London Times* and the *New York Times* and a few other newspapers and popular magazines back to 1900."

"Not bad for a small operation."

"There's a bequest from the museum founders that funds it."

"So where are you going to start?"

Julia considered. "Well, we know that Zoey Zander bought it from the Bertram Page auction."

"Bertram Page, the philanthropist?"

"You know any others? He didn't loan it out with any of his collections, as far as I know. I think Zoey bought it for the legend, as much as anything."

"Right. Good luck for the pure of heart." Alex gave her a bland look. "You want me to look that part up in the newspaper index, pure of heart?"

"Cute. You could see what you find on the White Star or Bertram Page."

"Right away, ma'am."

"I'll check the archives of the *Journal of Antiquities* and *American Curator* and see if I can find out who Page bought it from." She brought up the index and began hunting through it for references. With a little surge of triumph she found the name. "Okay, Zoey Zander bought the White Star from Page in 1994, it looks like. Both names show up anyway. Let me just verify that." She clicked and brought up the PDF for that issue.

Up popped the cover image, a photo of a stone fertility god with an erection half the size of his body. "Well, that gives a new meaning to 'hard as a rock,'" Alex observed over her shoulder. "So, let me guess, you just read it for the articles?"

Julia grinned. "Hell no, I get it for the centerfolds," she said and clicked around the PDF file.

Zoey Zander had been a collector. She'd collected houses, greyhounds, husbands and jewels, in roughly that order. If a piece was ostentatious, that was a start. If it had a scandalous history, so much the better. She loved nothing more than sporting an enormous rock and telling stories. After she'd bought the White Star, though, she'd been curiously private about it.

Almost as though it had been a treasure she'd wanted to keep to herself.

For the pure of heart. Julia snorted. Pure, Zoey Zander was not. She skimmed the auction news column at the back of the issue. "It looks like Page got the White Star from the estate of a Hollywood director named Foster Clark in 1954, who'd owned it since 1941."

"I'm on Foster," Alex said, flipping through the volume of the newspaper index.

It seemed archaic in this day and age to have old-fashioned hard-copy indices. Even microfilm seemed low-tech. The museum had made the investment, though, and saw no need to spend the money on upgrading resources that worked just fine.

Alex stepped over to the wide metal cabinets of microfilm and searched out the right roll. He switched on the reader that sat on the table next to her. "Okay if I turn down the lights so I can see better?"

"Sure," Julia said absently, going back through her own sources. When the room went dim, she jolted. "I didn't say turn them all off."

"I work better in the dark," Alex said in her ear, making her jump. She caught the flash of his teeth as he straightened and stepped over to sit at the microfilm reader next to her. "Is your chair comfortable?" he asked idly as he slouched in front of his machine.

She glanced down and heat flushed through her. She'd sat in it mere hours earlier, she thought, closing her eyes as she remembered the feel of his mouth on her, his hands on her, his cock sliding in and out. *You won't be able to resist....*

"Okey, dokey," Alex said. "Got the obit for Foster Clark. Director of more than a dozen films. Got an Oscar nomination in 1949 for *Long Day's Journey into Night.* Oh, wow." He stopped.

"What?"

"Clark was hauled in front of the House Un-American Activities Committee in 1952," he said slowly. "Joined the Communist Party in college. He couldn't start naming names fast enough. Not that it did him any good. He got blacklisted anyway, and took more than a few people down with him. Put a bullet in his brain in 1954."

Julia shivered. "I thought the White Star was a good-luck charm."

"For the pure of heart, remember?"

"So the report just says he bought the White Star in 1941. It doesn't say who from." She began sifting through the auction reports for 1941 and the years immediately following. Time slipped by in the artificial twilight of the darkened room; it was as though they were immersed in another world, diving into the past, looking at names and faces of people long gone.

Finally, she found what she was looking for. "Bennett Hastings," she said aloud. "Look for an obit, because the sale was by his estate."

"Consider it done."

But who, she wondered, had Hastings gotten it from?

And why was it the amulet seemed to always change hands because someone had died?

"God, I love microfilm," Alex said. "People look so bizarre in all the photos, like they're albinos. Okay, here's something on Hastings." He scanned the article. "Huh."

"What?"

"Forget about the obit. We need to look for a less…official source. I think there's dirt to dish on this guy."

"'Hastings Electronics heir, CEO,'" Julia read. "How do you figure?"

He pointed. "Keep reading. He became president and CEO of the company in 1938, when his father died. Hastings would have been thirty-one. By 1940, the company was in receivership. That's what's off. You don't run a company into the ground in less than two years on clean living." With the controls of the microfilm reader he rolled back through the issue to the entertainment pages and nodded in satisfaction. "'The Candle That Burned Too Brightly: the Life and Death of Bennett Hastings.' Thought so."

"What does it say?"

"Polo, gambling, summers in Monte Carlo. A paternity suit that got hushed up—with a maid, no less. Oh, our boy was quite a prize."

Julia scooted her chair closer to his. "But he paid for it in the end, it looks like."

"Yeah. Pasting yourself all over the side of a mountain is an ugly way to go. Good reminder not to drink and drive. He was under investigation by the Feds, although they don't say what for."

"Does it say anything about the amulet?" She leaned in toward Alex to get a better look at the text.

"This is cozy," he commented, slipping an arm around her. "I told you you couldn't resist me."

"I'm trying to do research," she muttered, shifting away.

"The couple who researches together, stays together."

"We're not a couple," she reminded him and went back to her own screen. They weren't a couple, although he was being surprisingly good company. None of the prowling restlessness she'd have guessed in such a situation. And the fact that he was helping her...

But it was a hopeless task, tracking the White Star back over thousands of years, especially with the resources she had. Like trying to find a needle in a haystack. What could possibly make her think she stood a chance?

"Got more on our bad boy Hastings, here," Alex said aloud, making her jump. "He used to hang out with some shady types, a gangster named Ray 'Legs' Legrande."

"Charming. That must have been the reason the Feds were looking into him."

"Could be."

"You know, it's a complete long shot but I just remembered that the first time I talked to Zoey about the amulet—the only time, actually—she said something about the White Star being owned by a bootlegger. Just for kicks..." She did a quick search. "Okay, there's an article here that comes up on Ray Legrande, called 'Art and Incarceration.' It looks like an editorial." She changed disks and brought up the file. "Interesting."

"What you got?"

She cleared her throat. "'What do we do when masterpieces and one-of-a-kind treasures wind up in the hands of criminals, bought by dirty money?'" she read aloud. "'Two years ago, Ray Legrande acquired the White Star amulet, an artifact known to date from at least 1000 B.C. Now, he's in federal court, facing racketeering charges. If convicted, he could be facing up to seventy years in prison. Whither then, White Star, managed by crooked lawyers, dubious heirs...' Etcetera, etcetera, etcetera."

Alex stirred. "What's the date?"

"Nineteen thirty-one."

"I think we need to find out a little more about Mr. Legrande." He rose. "I'll get that. You see if you can find where he got it from."

Time slid by with the click of the mouse, the whisper of pages, the whir of the microfilm reader as Alex searched for citations. And then...

"Score."

"I've got it."

They blinked at each other. "You first," Julia said.

"Bachelor number three, Ray 'Legs' Legrande."

"Why did they call him Legs?"

"It says here that in the early days he used to tell his victims to dance and he'd shoot at their feet before he started aiming higher. Then he moved up in the world and started having other people do the shooting for him."

"Nice." Julia read over his shoulder. "He worked out of Miami, huh? That'd be convenient if you were doing import/export, I'm guessing. What would someone like that want with the amulet?"

Alex scrubbed his knuckles against his jaw. "Apparently, he got the idea it, uh, enhanced potency. You worry about those kinds of things when you've got a young mistress."

"Life before Viagra."

"I'll just point out for the record, I've lived my life amulet-free."

"Duly noted. Read, please?"

"Let's see. 'Legrande had successfully ducked Federal prosecution when he was gunned down in what was believed to have been an underworld killing. The coroner removed twenty-eight bullets from his body, just a few more than the number of men he was reputed to have killed.' Guess he wasn't pure of heart," Alex said. "I don't know, the more I find out, the more I think our thief is welcome to the amulet."

"It didn't sound like any of these people needed help from the White Star, if that's even what it was. It sounds like they got what they deserved."

He clicked his tongue. "You're so judgmental."

"I'm not going to feel sorry that a man who shot twenty-some-odd people got killed. I mean, what about them? What about their families?"

Alex tilted his head. "Julia's got a sense of justice."

"I just don't like seeing bad things happen to people."

He brushed a finger over her chin. "Nice."

The touch shivered through her. For a moment, she just looked at him. In the dimness his face was all planes and angles. There was a special intensity to the shadowed eyes. He didn't look like the smiling, happy-go-lucky Alex that she knew. He looked like someone else suddenly, a man capable of much more.

"So what did you find out?"

Julia blinked. "What?" She gave her head a brisk shake, groping for a lucid thought. "Oh, um, it says here that he bought it at auction from a divorcée named Lillian Bashford. It doesn't say anything about her."

Alex flipped open the newspaper index. "Bashford, Bashford, Bashford…" He shot her a devilish look. "Five will get you ten there's a story there. I'll bet you a carnal act I find it first."

"Dream on."

"About the carnal act or winning the bet?" he asked, slamming shut the index and rising to get the microfilm.

"Both," she shot back, fingers already flying. "'Bashford, Lillian, Auction Update,'" she read in satisfaction and pulled out the CD-ROM. Next to her, Alex was threading the new roll of film into the reader.

The PDF took a while to open, courtesy of the Stone Age computer that had wound up in the basement by default. Julia drummed her fingers, listening to the whir of the microfilm reader as Alex scanned the roll at warp speed, trying to get to the right page.

Julia clicked on the file to find her way to the article. And stared. It was a photograph of the amulet. "Alex," she said faintly. "Here it is. 'Sold, as part of a private auction by Lillian Bashford, the White Star amulet, carved ivory and carnelian, circa 1050 B.C.'"

"'Hit by the crash of the stock market, Lillian Bashford has put up her entire collection of jewelry for auction,'" Alex read. "Oh, hey, listen to this. 'Pieces include a number of valuable items she received in the settlement from her ex-husband, Aubrey Fitz-Lewis, Earl of Ashbroke. Society watchers will recall the bitter divorce proceedings in which Fitz-Lewis contended that Bashford was claiming items considered part of the Fitz-Lewis family jewels, including an ancient Egyptian amulet.'"

"So she took poor Aubrey for everything he had," Julia mused, "and then wound up losing it all in the crash. Now that's karma."

"Don't feel too bad for old Aubrey. Sounds like he took her, too. 'Bashford filed court documents showing that she'd poured over five hundred thousand dollars into propping up Fitz-Lewis's failing family estate....' Not chump change, especially back then," Alex added. "'Divorce was granted on the grounds of infidelity.' Sounds like they were quite a pair."

Julia skimmed her auction item, hoping for a description of the White Star she could conclusively match to the object she'd seen. She heard Alex come up behind her.

"So, do I get that carnal act?"

"No way, I found the mention first."

"You found the auction," he corrected. "You didn't find the scoop on Lillian and Aubrey."

She gave him a pat on the cheek. "You are so dreaming."

He caught at her hand. "You touched me voluntarily."

"So?"

"I told you you'd break down eventually."

She snorted. "Now you're really dreaming."

"Speaking of which, has it occurred to you that if security doesn't show, we've got another problem on our hands?"

"Besides food?"

"Yeah. Where the hell are we going to sleep?"

THE BAR WAS SHABBY AND DARK, tucked away on a back street, with bars on the windows. It was the type of place where a man didn't stand out, the sort of place people kept to themselves.

The sort of place Allard liked best.

He lifted the glass of amber liquid and drank, letting the fire of the cheap whiskey scorch his throat. Soon he would be able to afford better. Soon he would be drinking the finest of aged brandies. For now, though, he would take this, reward for a job well done. He set down the glass and slipped his hand into his pocket.

The White Star.

Slowly, carefully, he brought her out, cupping the ancient ivory in his hands. Even in the dim yellow light, she glowed. Even in the dim yellow light, she drew him. He couldn't stop staring. He couldn't stop touching. And when he held her, he almost felt a heat, almost a faint pulse.

It was just the whiskey making him soft headed. He shoved her back into his pocket. How his father would have sneered. The White Star was just a prize—a prize that would bring him a million euros, maybe more. Almost certainly more.

After all, he'd taken risks to recover her.

But he'd pulled off a nearly perfect job. The utilities room, so conveniently down the hall from the lovers. A few moments, only, to pull the necessary wires to shut off communications. He gave a faint smile and raised the glass to his lips. Such a pleasure, those professionals who carefully labeled each and every cable. A simple matter to pull every line marked Basement, and voilà, no inconvenient calls for help.

He wondered if the fools in the museum had even realized they were locked in yet, or whether they were merely still locked together, searching for release. The image of pale breasts, the sound of urgent moans rose in his mind. And the pale glow of the White Star. His fingers tightened around the glass. A woman. He needed one, and soon.

As soon as his prize was secured.

He slipped his hand back into his pocket. Tomorrow, he would put her in a safe place. Tomorrow, he would make plans. For tonight, he would simply enjoy.

Slowly, almost unwillingly, he brought out the amulet, cupping it in his palm, tracing a fingertip over the hole that pierced it through.

Tomorrow, he would negotiate her return to his client.

For tonight, she was his.

9

"WE DON'T NEED to worry about sleeping yet," Julia hedged. "It's not even eleven."

Alex raised an eyebrow. "You have to admit, it is an issue we're going to have to consider."

"I thought someone said that security was bound to come by and let us out."

"Did someone say that?" He stuck his tongue in his cheek. "Someone may have been wrong."

That was one thing she'd always appreciated about Alex—his relative lack of ego. Or insecurities, rather. Ego he had, in abundance. He was about the cockiest guy she'd ever met, but he wasn't one of those like Edward, who got angry and terse anytime he was questioned. Maybe Alex could be that way precisely because of his ego—because his sense of self was strong enough that admitting he was wrong wasn't the end of the earth.

"Do I pass inspection?" He watched her in amusement. "Or are you just fighting your undeniable attraction for me? Not to mention the fact that despite your best efforts, we're going to be sleeping together."

"Sleeping in the same room," she corrected. "Possibly."

"Our thief was a matchmaker. We'll have to invite him to the wedding."

"The one we'll be having in the mental institution where they put you for delusions?"

"Aha," he pounced. "You've admitted that we're going to have one. You're falling under my spell, hour by hour."

She snorted. "Yeah, right. Why don't you take your giant ego out to the main lab, assuming you can get your head through the door, and let me work?"

"No way. It's just getting good. Besides, you're going to need all the help you can get now. No more indexed newspapers to help out. Now it's getting trickier, like how did our Aubrey get his mitts on the White Star?"

"Assuming we're correct in thinking it was included when Lillian scooped his family jewels."

"Let's not get into her ugly physical retaliation," Alex said.

Julia rolled her eyes. "The *real* family jewels. Let's say, for a minute, that the 'Egyptian amulet' is actually the White Star. We have to assume it was a family heirloom."

"All the way from B.C.? That's some family." Alex studied the picture of Aubrey Fitz-Lewis they'd dug up. "He doesn't look Egyptian."

"It's not Egyptian, remember? We know it came from somewhere around there because it exhibits certain similarities in materials and workmanship and style, but it's not Egyptian."

"God, you get me hot when you talk dirty."

Her cheeks tinted. "You're making fun of me."

"No." His face was serious. "I mean it. There's nothing sexier than a smart woman."

It gave her a little flutter of pleasure inside. Edward had loved her intelligence, but only when it didn't show up his own. She'd always figured Alex for the type who'd rather hang out with a woman who didn't challenge him, who was undemanding. Maybe—clearly, she admitted to herself—she'd underestimated him.

On the other hand, he charmed people for a living. Maybe he was just saying what he thought she wanted to hear. *First rule of sales—figure out what I want and show me how the deal gives it to me.*

"So don't stop. It shares certain similarities...." Alex prompted.

"Uh, yes, it does. And all reports have it coming from ancient times, plus..."

"What?"

She flushed. "It'll sound silly."

"No. Tell me."

"It felt old. Something about it felt like it was from another time."

He didn't laugh, as she'd feared. Instead, his expression was sober. "I felt it, too."

"You didn't," she said, but she knew somehow that he was telling the truth.

"When I touched it. There was something." His gaze locked on hers.

The snap of connection was sudden and shocking, as it had been when he'd touched the amulet. For a moment, it was as though he were staring into her soul and she into his, and what she saw was far more complex than she'd ever imagined.

"What brought you here?" she blurted.

He gave her a puzzled look. "What?"

"Why did you come here?"

"The museum or New York?" he responded, bemused.

"The museum. Why did you come to work here?" She'd never asked. It hadn't been a part of the world they'd created for themselves. And suddenly she was eager to know.

Alex shrugged. "After I got my undergrad degrees, I knocked around for a couple of years. Chicago, mostly. That's where I'm from. I tried brokering, did some low-level management. None of it was really my thing, so I went back for an MBA."

"When in doubt, go to school?"

"Watch what you say there. My parents are teachers."

"No kidding?"

"Yeah. My mom teaches English at a prep school and my dad's a philosophy prof at Northwestern."

It was the first time he'd ever talked about his background, she realized. He'd known about hers from the beginning. Not that she'd ever told him, but word got around about that sort of thing, especially when her family—and occasionally, embarrassingly, she—showed up in the social pages.

"Do you like them?" she asked without thinking.

"Yeah, I do. And they gave me a good example—the more you know, the more choices you have. One thing leads to another. During my MBA, I interned at the Art Institute of Chicago. Did a thesis on new fund-raising structures for nonprofits. The Institute liked it so much they hired me for real."

"Did you like living in Chicago?"

"I grew up in Evanston, which was okay. I loved living in the city, though. The music scene is just amazing."

"Why did you leave?"

He didn't answer right away but turned a roll of microfilm over and over in his hands. "I don't know," he said finally. "After a while I felt like I was just going through the motions, you know? Everything was too easy. I wanted something that…challenged me, I guess. If that doesn't sound pretentious."

That stopped her. It wasn't the Alex she knew, the

guy who made a big show of skating along, of bobbling through life like a bit of bark floating in a river. "I thought you liked easy."

Frustration flared in his eyes. "God, I am so sick of hearing that. I worked my ass off to get here and I bring in a lot of money for this museum. You want to tell me why everybody thinks I'm some kind of slacker who never gets anything done?"

"Hey, relax," she said, taken aback. "I wasn't trying to insult you. It's just that, I don't know, you always sort of seem like you're just coasting along. Like it's all a big joke."

"So I'm not allowed to have a good time while I'm getting the job done?"

She took a breath. "That's not what I mean," she said carefully. "But the reality is, if you act like you don't take anything seriously, people are going to believe it. That's not a statement on your competence, it's just the way it is."

"Even you?"

Now it was her turn for impatience. "Alex, think about how we've spent our time before now. You seemed like the guy out for a good time, which was okay because I was, too. I just figured that was all there was to it—and to you."

"And now?" His gaze was steady on hers.

She shifted uncomfortably. "I don't know. The jury's still out."

"Scratch below the surface, Julia," he said softly.

"I know." The moment stretched out, and before she realized she was going to do it, she found herself reaching out for his hand. She caught herself in time, though, and instead rubbed at a speck of imaginary dust on the computer screen. "Anyway, we've got a job to do. We need to figure out how the amulet got from the desert to the UK."

Alex relaxed, letting the discussion go. For the time being. She had an uncomfortable feeling it was going to come back up again before they were through. And she didn't know what her answer was going to be.

"Right," he said. "Colonial acquisition? You know those Brits, they packed up half of Egypt when they were first over there. They could have scooped up the amulet and taken it home. Maybe one of Fitz-Lewis's ancestors was an explorer, or an officer in the army."

"Could be, but it doesn't feel right."

"What does that mean?"

She rolled her shoulders. "I don't know. I've just got a feeling that it made its way one step at a time, and if we track it, we'll find out how."

"You've got a feeling? My very proper, academic Julia?"

"Scratch beneath the surface, Alex."

He pursed his lips. "Hoist on my own petard."

"Damned right," she agreed.

"You've got to admit, it's a fetching petard, though."

Her lips twitched. "So let's track the Fitz-Lewises, see if we can find out more about them. Maybe the Earl of Ashbroke has some secrets." Julia glanced at him, and did a double take, noticing his frown. "What?"

"That name. Something about it rings a bell."

"Fitz-Lewis?"

"Ashbroke."

"You mean in a historic sense?"

"I don't know. Maybe I just saw a mention of the modern-day earl somewhere. It could be just the name of a hotel or a town, for that matter. I wish we had access to the Internet."

"You and me both," she said ruefully.

Alex rose. "I've got to go see a man about a dog anyway. I'll stop in and check what's-his-face's—"

"Paul's."

"Paul's laptop. Maybe the network is back up."

"You were talking about sleep earlier. Are you ready to call it a night? Because you don't have to keep going. You can stop if you want to."

The surprise on his face was genuine. "Do you?"

She shook her head. "I'm not tired. I'm going to keep chugging away. I just thought you might want to take a break."

"Why? We're just getting somewhere. Hell, what else am I going to do, talk about the Yankee game with Felix? Come on, let's do it. Do you have some kind of peerage reference here? *Burke's* or something?"

"How do you know about *Burke's?*" she asked, surprised.

He grinned. "With a history degree and a name like Spencer, I have to answer that?"

"Well. It's a good idea."

"I know." He gave her a devilish look. "Now about that carnal act…"

She shooed him out the door. "Go see about your dog. What you do in privacy is your own business."

"GOOD LORD," Julia said, staring at the peerage book. "How many of them were there?"

"A lot. Some fertile people, those Lewises. Particularly when they added the hyphenate."

She skimmed the pages spread open before them. "So I guess we're not likely to come across anything like a note that one of them was an explorer, or collected art."

"You're cute when you're optimistic," Alex said, tweaking her nose. "The kind of stuff you want would be in a family history, and there's no way you're going to have something like that in this room. Burke's Peerage is only going to give you births, deaths, marriages, titles, that sort of thing."

"I just wish they had details."

"Hey, they've got details. Look at this, 'Lord William Fitz-Lewis, entered military service in 1808 as Ensign, 44th Foot, served in Belgium, 1814.' Oh, hell, Waterloo," Alex burst out, snapping his fingers. "That's where I knew it from. The Earl of Ashbroke. He commanded a regiment at the Battle of Waterloo. Cavalry. He kept a fairly famous journal of the campaign. Any chance you'd have that here?"

"We might. We have some personal accounts. Let me look." She brought up the library index and typed in the name. A few seconds ticked by and the information scrolled on screen. "Robert Fitz-Lewis, Earl of Ashbroke," she read. "It's shelved in the—"

"I've got it." He rose. "You turn the lights back up."

The journal, when he brought it, proved to be thinner than she'd expected. Alex sat beside her and started paging through it.

"First printed in 1834, reprinted in 1915 to celebrate the hundredth anniversary of Waterloo. Look, here's Earl." Alex pointed to a frontis engraving of an officer on horseback, silver braid chasing across the blue of his tunic, his long, thick sideburns trailing down the side of his face below his tall, black hat.

"Pretty fancy outfit."

"Better than my petard?"

"Your petard is in a class of its own. So how are we going to do this?"

"You could hang on me adoringly and read over my shoulder," Alex suggested.

"Next?"

"We could sit side by side and each read one side of the spread at the same time. Look at it as a team-building exercise."

Julia flicked a glance at the ceiling and stood. "Maybe I'll go see if you harmed that dog."

"Careful," Alex said. "He bites."

10

"ASHBROKE, YOU ROCK."

Julia jumped at the sound of Alex's exclamation in the silence. She'd come back to the repository and begun combing through the previous sources for more images of the amulet, letting Alex read through Ashbroke's journal. Now, it appeared, he'd found something.

"Listen to this." His voice was filled with barely suppressed excitement. "It's from after the battle, when the army was marching to Paris to stick a fork in old Napoleon. 'Being somewhat impatient and in high spirits, we chose a road apart from the main army, traveling with some haste, if only to create a breeze to temper the warmth of the day. We passed through a small village known as St. Denis, named for the handsome abbey beyond, so said a young lad of whom I inquired. We passed along peacefully enough until, some few miles farther along, a woman's shriek pierced the air.

"'Launching into full gallop, we topped a rise and came upon a scene of fearful confusion. Below lay a modest manor house and farm, flames blazing from the thatch of the barn, while the blood of a fresh-killed swine ran in the dirt of the yard. All round rode the members of a company of Prussian soldiers, those devils bent on punishing all France for their treatment at Bonaparte's hands. Some were gathering up chickens and tying them across their saddles. An old man and three children stood fearfully against a wall, whilst some of the villains trained muskets on them, bent upon grave mischief. The other soldiers held a woman among them. It was she who was screaming.

"'I can scarce describe the fury that the sight ignited in me. That they were allies mattered not. I would not dignify such scoundrels with the name. I discharged my pistol into the air to capture their attention and we rode into their midst with dispatch. It was the work of but moments to take into custody the officers of the group and the soldiers, for such men are cowards when faced with any but the weak. In truth, I found myself sorely tempted to hang them all, but instead asked for them to be properly guarded for delivery to the authorities when we should arrive in Paris. In the meantime, I set my men to extinguish the fire and bring such order as they could to the scene.

"'We searched the Prussians, and not gently, and upon their captain I discovered a broach and some rings and other booty, all wrapped in a handkerchief. He had been looting alongside his men, I understood, taking such valuables as the family owned before burning the farm to the ground.

"'I approached the woman, who was giving comfort to her boys. She was dark-eyed and young, in the gravest of distress, clearly, and yet meeting my eye with a self-possession remarkable in the face of all that had transpired. Her English was passable, far exceeding my French. Her husband was gone to battle, she said, and the Prussians had come upon them and laid waste all 'round. It was then that I espied the bruise upon her cheek and the rents in her skirts. I fear I lost my temper then and pistol-whipped the Prussian captain quite bloody.

"'When I had finished, I made to apologize to the woman for all she had suffered, though it seemed far inadequate on the face of it. On the contrary, she said, we had delivered them of an evil fate. She was the daughter of the lord of these lands in the years prior to the revolution, after which their fortunes had suffered. The jewels meant much to her, for they were a reminder of better days and some small insurance of comfort in the event of ill times. She bade me take something for my pains and would hear none of my protests but pressed an object upon me.

"'And so I looked at it and felt a curious stillness come over me. It was not, as I had feared, a jewel but an amulet of ivory, with points all round. It had been a charm of good fortune to their family for more than two hundred years, she said, and had been blessed by men of God. It had not come from France; indeed, I sensed it had not come from Europe at all, but from some land of mysterious tongues and foreign winds, far, far from here.

"'It rests now in front of me as I sit here, writing. It is not a beautiful object to place alongside the jewels I drape about my lady's throat, and yet there is something about it that compels me, something I cannot name. There is a grace to it, a presence; more, I cannot say. I should not have taken it from the young woman.

"'But I know I will keep this thing, old and cracked though it may be.'"

"Oh, my God, the crack." Julia snatched up the folder of drawings and photographs of the amulet she'd brought in, flipping through it frantically. "Look, here." She pointed to the hairline crack in her sketch. "You can't see it in the photograph, but it's right there on the back. It's the same amulet. She gave him the White Star. And he held on to it for a while. Assuming it was the White Star to begin with."

"Boy, you're tough to convince. Let's see if he says anything else about it." Alex skimmed through the pages.

"Alex," Julia said thoughtfully, "have you noticed that when the good guys get the White Star, they keep it, but when the bad guys get it, they seem to die not too soon after? I mean, Page owned it for forty years. Ashbroke's family held it for nearly a hundred."

"That's because he was pure of heart. Not to mention good at kicking Prussian butt. And the French woman said that her family had had the amulet for two hundred years."

"So?" Alex asked.

"So if her family held it for two hundred years, maybe they got it honorably."

"Like how?"

"I don't know. We don't even know their name." She fell silent. "What was that line about a blessing?"

Alex ran his finger down the page. "Right here, it 'had been blessed by men of God.'" He glanced at her. "Are you thinking the abbey?"

"That's where we go next. Maybe they made a gift of it to the lord or gave it to him in exchange for land or protection or whatever."

Alex rubbed his eyes. "Can the going next happen tomorrow? All this channeling of aristocrats is exhausting."

Julia rose with him. "Of course. It's nearly one anyway. I just get caught up in this stuff. It's fascinating, don't you think? I mean, seeing it through the eyes of a person who was there. It makes it so real."

Enthusiasm bubbled in her voice. Alex glanced at her as they walked out into the main lab. "Why antiquities then? You seem to really connect with European history and art. Actually, why work at all, for that matter? You're rich, aren't you? You could study this in your free time, do what you want with your life."

"I am doing what I want with my life." Now, she sounded prickly. "I love European art and history, but everyone does it. I don't know, I've always felt something for antiquities. The idea of anything being that old, I guess, of civilization being that old." She picked up one of the empty soda cans and rinsed it out at the sink. "When I was a girl, I used to spend an afternoon every other week with my great-aunt Stella, who was just wonderful. One day she took me to the Met." She filled the can with water.

"And you saw Felix and it was love at first sight."

She gave a faint smile. "It wasn't a mummy at all. It was a cup, a robin's-egg-blue glass cup. It had been in the ground for so many years, patches were covered with these iridescent rainbows. Really beautiful. I couldn't stop looking at it. And then we went to the museum café to get a snack. I picked up my water glass and all of a sudden I realized that it was just like the blue cup. Someone thousands of years ago had sat at a table, maybe, or cross-legged on cushions, and drunk from that glass, maybe a little girl like me. And maybe someone thousands of years from now would find my cup and wonder about me.

"And for the first time, I realized that people all those millennia ago were just people like us. And they became real to me." She smiled faintly. "I dragged Aunt Stella back there every week that whole summer. And I dreamed every night about the little girl."

There was a light in her eyes, as she talked, an openness that was entirely new. This was a Julia he'd never seen before. And he wanted more. "Now go back. Who was your aunt Stella? Is she one of the socialites?"

"Great-aunt Stella, actually. My grandmother's sister. And no, absolutely no. She was the family iconoclast. She went to Paris in the Forties after the war and lived with an artist, and then moved to San Francisco. She came back when my grandmother died and sort of took me under her wing. It was Aunt Stella who helped me get up the nerve to stand up to the rest of the family."

"Stand up to the rest of the family? So you're a rebel, Ms. I'm Really So Serious?"

Julia shifted. "No, right now I'm just tired," she said abruptly, setting the soda can aside. "Let's figure out what we're going to do about sleeping."

It hadn't been much, but for a short while she'd really talked to him about things that mattered to her. And he'd be as patient as he needed to be to see that it happened again. "Well, it looks to me like we've got three choices—chair, table or floor."

She surveyed him. "You honestly think you're going to be even remotely comfortable sleeping in a chair?"

"I said it was a choice. I didn't say it was a good one. The downside of the table is that you can always roll off."

"You must be a pretty sound sleeper," she observed. "Do you snore?"

"You'd know the answer to that if you'd ever spent the night. You do realize we're taking our relationship to a new level here?"

Julia gave him a look from under her brows. "We don't have a relationship, remember?"

"Oh, you can talk tough all you want, but I think you're getting a soft spot for me."

"Well, it's not big enough to sleep on, so don't get your hopes up." She stalked over to a utility closet and pulled out some plastic and tarps.

"What are those?"

"The nearest thing to something soft that we've got."

Alex helped her carry them over and begin folding them up. "They're certainly big enough for us to sleep on."

"I figured we'd make two separate pallets."

"You do it together, we'll have more cushioning. Besides," he tempted, "we can keep each other warm."

"It's not that cold in here."

"Says the woman who's always freezing. And you're not lying on a chilly floor. Trust me, body heat is a good thing."

"Trust you?" she echoed skeptically, but she laid the second folded tarp atop the first.

"I'm only thinking of your welfare. Besides, we've got a chaperone." He helped her lay the folded sheets of plastic in place, then set the tarps on top. "If I try anything funny, you can just call out for Felix to come to your rescue. Then again, being a thirty-five-hundred-year-old dead guy, he may just get ideas of his own. I mean, it's probably been a while."

Julia just rolled her eyes.

Alex started unbuttoning his shirt. "Well, I'm going to get comfortable," he said, slipping off his shoes. "Feel free to take off anything you like. I won't mind."

"Why am I not surprised?" Her voice was dry.

"Need some help?" he offered. "Anything you can't reach?"

She couldn't quite stop the smile. "I'm all set, thanks."

"Don't say I never offered."

"I wouldn't dream of it."

He picked up his suit coat and folded it in half, then handed it to her. "Pillow."

"Alex, you don't have to—"

"Ladies first. I'll use it tomorrow night."

"With any luck, we won't be here tomorrow night."

"I'll still use it." He squinted at the door and pushed a couple of chairs aside, then glanced over at Julia. "Okay, lights-out time. Better get into your bunk or the camp counselor's going to be really mad."

She smiled and laid down on the pallet. The darkness, when it hit, was complete. She heard the rustling of Alex working his way back toward her.

"Is that you or Felix?"

"Me. Although Felix might be bringing up the rear," he added, sinking down onto the pallet beside her. "You never know. Keep an ear out for noises."

Julia laughed. "Good night, Alex." And then stiffened as he reached out to pull her against him.

"Body heat, remember?"

"I'm not that cold yet."

"All the better to plan ahead."

The spooning felt nice, she realized. Comforting. "Alex?"

"Yes?" he murmured in her ear.

"Thanks for the pillow."

"Don't mention it."

She heard a little rustle of plastic. "Is that you?"

His laugh rumbled. "I think it's Felix. He's ticked off he got left out. Wants to know where Nefertiti is."

"Tell him we'll fix him up with a nice little queen up-stairs."

"I'll do that."

The room fell silent. "Alex?" Julia said again.

"Hmm?"

"Thanks for being so nice about all of this. It could have been really awkward to be locked in together. You've made it as easy as possible."

"T'weren't nothin', little lady," he murmured. "Sweet dreams."

There was another little rustle of plastic.

With a smile, Julia closed her eyes.

AND JULIA DREAMED of the desert....

The evening wind whisked over the land like a hot sigh, a wind that had come many miles. It wasn't the shrieking wail of the sandstorms but the heated breath that reminded her of the vastness that lay beyond the palms.

She crouched now with her best friend and watched the caravan draw near to the oasis, the dun-colored camels striding along with their rolling gait. What did they bring from so far away, the white robed traders with their turbans? What lay in their coffers?

Her friend had eyes only for the scimitars that hung at the belts of the warriors who guarded the caravan. "I'll carry a sword like that one day," he pronounced.

"And I'll wear the jewels of the caravan, and ride on a white camel and you can protect me," she said.

"Of course," he said grandly, "I'll fight off the desert hordes for you, an entire army with just one man, and my name will be famous throughout the kingdom."

"And will you still be my friend?" she asked.

"Always," he said.

11

IT HAD BEEN TOO LONG since he had been with a woman, Allard thought as he stared at the young blonde behind the desk. She glanced down at the contract before her. "And what size safe-deposit box did you need, Mr. Allen?"

"John, please," he said, smiling at her. "The four-by-five box will do."

"That will be eighty-eight dollars for the year. At the end of that time, you'll receive papers to renew the box if you choose."

He would not need to renew, of course. He would not even need the box for a year. For two nights, though, he would rest more easily knowing the White Star was safe. Ironic that he who had broken into so many vaults would choose one for safekeeping, but he needed a woman and he would not risk having the White Star while he did.

"I'll just need some identification," the blonde said.

He handed her a passport and she made an apologetic moue. "I'm sorry, but with a passport, we need a second form of ID."

"Certainly," he looked at her name badge, "Caroline."

She flushed. He reached into the breast pocket of his elegant suit to pull out his wallet. So careful, so cautious, these petty bureaucrats, and all the time he danced around them, doing as he chose. Did they think that asking for additional papers could stop him? To a clever forger with resources, one document was much like the next, and for a price, anything could be had.

He passed over his driver's license, a license identifying him as John Allen, resident of Fort Lee, New Jersey.

The bank clerk clicked away at her computer, studying the screen before filling in numbers on the contract and turning to him. "Now, if you'll just sign here, and also sign your access card, that will complete the paperwork."

The pen he pulled out was a Montblanc, of course. People were so easily duped. When they saw what they expected to see, they asked no questions.

He signed the forms with a flourish.

"Excellent. Now here's your key. All you have to do is show that card and you can access your box anytime we're open. Would you like to get into it now?"

"I would, chérie."

She pinkened again. "If you'll just follow me into the vault," she said.

"But of course," he said and rose.

Inside the vault, the fluorescent lights gleamed down on the tiled floor. Around him rose the ranks of safe-deposit boxes. There were precious things entombed all around him; he could smell them. And if he wanted, he could return by night and take whatever he chose. It would not be the first occasion he'd done such a thing. But now was not the time for distractions, and soon, very soon, he would no longer need to steal precious things.

He would be able to buy whatever he wished.

His White Star would buy it for him.

JULIA OPENED her eyes to blackness. For an instant she tensed, before memory flooded back and she realized where she was. In the outside world, the light of dawn indicated morning. In the tomblike black of the conservation lab, it might have been midnight, it might have been midafternoon. She couldn't say. She knew only that she was conscious.

She stared across the room, willing her eyes to adjust. Rising, she groped for the lab bench that she knew was near. And then, finally, she could see the faint strip of light from the bottom of the laboratory door. Suddenly, as though it had snapped to a grid, the room took shape in her mind and she knew where she stood.

She let out a breath she was barely aware of holding.

"Weird, isn't it?" a voice asked.

She jumped. "Alex?"

"Yeah. I'm glad you're up. Let's get the lights on."

She heard his quick, sure footsteps heading toward the door and she understood his insistence the night before on moving workbenches and chairs. Leaving a clear path to the light switch, she realized.

And with a click he turned on the lights. "Good morning."

"Coffee," she rasped, squinting at the brightness.

"What?"

"I can't function without coffee." At home, it brewed while she showered and was ready by the time she began dressing. And suddenly the full horror of the situation sank in. Not only were they locked in, they were locked in without caffeine. "Is there any Coke left?" she asked, trying to keep the desperation from her voice.

"I can do better," he said smugly. "Depending on how grateful you're prepared to be."

"What's that supposed to mean?"

"How much do you want coffee?"

She glowered at him. "If you're teasing me, I will have to hurt you."

He shook his head at her sorrowfully. "This is so disappointing, Julia. I never knew you were like this in the mornings."

"Now aren't you glad we never actually spent the night together all those nights?"

"I might be," he agreed, walking over to duck into Paul's office. "Then again, if coffee soothes the savage beast, then it's coffee you will get." He stepped out holding an automatic coffeemaker.

Julia stared. "Tell me you have coffee for that," she said faintly.

Alex whipped a bag of coffee out from behind his back with a flourish. "Ta da. And filters."

"Don't take this the wrong way, but I think I may be in love with you," she told him.

Alex's grin widened. "Are you prepared to demonstrate that love?"

She took the machine from him. "I meant only in the platonic sense. You know, that pure-of-heart thing."

"Relax, the amulet's not around. I'll take impure. I'd be quite happy with impure."

She added a filter and coffee in the upper trap. "And I'm quite happy with this," she crooned, pouring in the water. "I know he's not supposed to have that here and I know he breaks the rules anytime he wants, but I think you should know that right now, I love Paul, too."

"In the pure or the impure sense?"

Julia took a blissful sniff. "In every sense."

"I'd be jealous if that didn't smell so damned good." Alex walked over to the sink with a mug. "By the way, I hunted around and there's no sugar or anything. So in the words of the immortal Henry Ford, you can have any type of coffee you want as long as it's black."

"I don't care," she said, drumming her fingers on the counter until she could snatch out the pot and pour a cup. It took a half dozen swallows before she opened her eyes back up.

Only to find Alex watching her with amusement. "Welcome back," he said, leaning against a table. "Let's start again. The year is 2006."

"Good morning." She smiled. "What time is it?"

"Oh, a quarter of nine or so."

"A quarter of nine?" Her eyes widened. "I never sleep that late."

"I tend to wear women out," he observed.

"How'd you sleep?"

He shrugged. "It reminded me of why I never liked camping when I was in Boy Scouts."

"You were a Boy Scout?"

"Only for as long as it took me to go on my first camping trip."

Coffee proved the fact that there really was better living through chemistry. She also discovered that she missed a toothbrush and toothpaste far more than she'd missed a bed and pillow; water and her finger were hardly a substitute. "What we need now is for one of these people to be a dental-hygiene freak and keep toothpaste in their tool bench."

"I can't help you there, but I do have some of those breath strips," Alex offered.

Julia gave the little flat green plastic pack he held out a dubious look. "I've never had one of these."

"Try it, you'll like it," he said genially.

She pulled one of the little green strips out and inspected it. "It looks like plastic." She put the sheet on her tongue and screwed up her face. "That has to be the nastiest thing I've ever tasted." She took a hurried swallow of water from her soda can.

"It makes you feel remotely human, though, doesn't it?"

Julia rubbed her tongue against her teeth. "I think I've just replaced one foul taste with another, but I suppose it's a slight improvement." She let out a breath. "Well, happy Saturday. You think we've got a chance of getting out today?"

"I wouldn't count on it." He looked at her soberly. "Unless one of the conservators comes in for some weekend work, I'd plan on being stuck until Monday."

"Oh, great," Julia groaned. "That's just great."

"Cheer up. Maybe if we look around we can find some more mummy flesh to eat."

"That's not the point. I'm supposed to be at the gala tonight."

"Sorry, darlin'. I think we've tried everything we can try."

"But it's an important event. My mother's important event." And if Julia wasn't there, there was going to be hell to pay.

"Hey." Alex brightened. "Do you think they'd call the cops, maybe come looking for you?"

Julia sighed. "No, she'll just think I blew it off and be furious and completely hurt."

"Once we're out, though, you can explain."

"You don't know my mother."

"Uh-oh, do we need a bottle of wine for this?"

"If there's wine in that refrigerator, then I *am* going after Paul's behind."

And that quickly, that deftly, she turned the conversation away from herself.

Alex suppressed the little surge of frustration. He

should be used to it by now. It was the same blank wall he always came up against. The minute things became personal, Julia adroitly found a way to elude, evade. Escape.

Escaping wasn't going to be so easy now, though, he thought. The night before had shown that. She had nowhere to go, there was nothing to distract either of them. Given enough time, he might just make it past those barriers she'd erected.

He bounced on his toes, restless. Normally at this hour he'd be working out, running in Central Park or hitting the palatial facilities of the health club at the Chelsea Piers. Now, of course, he was trapped in the lab.

Shrugging, he slipped off his socks and began pulling off his T-shirt. He saw Julia's head snap around toward him, but she said nothing. Then his hands dropped to his belt.

She gave him a sardonic look. "Trying out for Chippendales?"

Was it his imagination or did she sound just the least bit uneasy? Interesting, considering how many times they'd been naked together. He pulled down his zipper, taking his time, watching her eyes widen as he pushed down his trousers.

And then her mild alarm gave way to amusement. She eyed his boxers. "Palm trees?"

"Just my fun-loving nature."

"If stripping is a way of hinting that you want to have sex, you'd be barking up the wrong palm tree."

"But I thought you said you loved me," he protested.

"I refuse to be held accountable for anything I say before coffee."

Alex ignored her and stepped out of his trousers.

Julia folded her arms. "Do you have nudist persuasions I'm not aware of?"

He grinned. "Nope." He dropped down and began to do push-ups. "Just feeling a little stir-crazy. I thought I'd see if I could work some of it off." The muscles flexed in his arms and torso.

Julia just stared.

He turned his head a little to glance at her. "You can help out by keeping count if you want."

Nineteen...twenty...twenty-one... Her brain feverishly kept up the count as he worked. She was powerless to turn away. His triceps flexed, his pecs swelled. She'd seen him naked before, but not like this, not outside of the flash and fire of lovemaking when she couldn't think straight. Now, she could just look.

His body was long, stripped down, muscled but not muscle-bound. It was the kind of build that was an adventure for the hands, all dips and rises, smooth curves and intriguing hollows.

She remembered.

Thirty-nine...forty...forty-one... She watched him move and thought of sliding her hands over him. She watched him tense and thought of how his body clenched at orgasm. She watched him dip and she couldn't help but imagine his body stretched over hers, skin pressed to skin, against her, on her, in her, sliding, rubbing, thrusting, slick, heavy, hot, hard.

"Fifty." Breathing easily, Alex got to his feet. He looked at her more closely. "You okay? You have seen a person do push-ups before, right?"

It would be too obvious if she shoveled her tongue back into her mouth with her hands, Julia thought. "Of course. I've just never seen it done in palm trees before."

A corner of his mouth curved up. "It's important to

broaden your horizons." He walked to the end of the gantry and hopped up to catch the crossbar. And before her stupefied gaze he began doing pull-ups.

This was worse than the push-ups, far worse. She watched the swell of his biceps, the flare of his lats, watched his body move as easily as though it were a machine that knew no fatigue, no limits.

"If you're going to stare, you're going to have to start counting for me," he grunted.

Julia flushed. "I'm not staring."

"Really? What do you call it then?"

"I'm monitoring your safety so that I can react if the gantry breaks and dumps you on your butt."

"That's neighborly of you." He was breathing harder now, she noticed, although given that he was up to nearly twenty, she didn't blame him.

"I grew up in a public-service-oriented family."

He dropped lightly to the ground and dusted off his hands. "I'm sure they'd be proud of you." He walked over to get a drink.

It had grown warmer in the room, Julia realized, and unbuttoned the bottom button of her jacket.

"Are you thinking about joining me?" Alex asked. "Or are you just getting warm?"

"Exercise is a spectator sport for me." She pushed up her sleeves. "You seem to be doing fine on your own."

"It's lonely."

"I'm sure you'll survive."

"Guess I'll just have to work out my frustrations." And he took two steps toward the wall and swung up into a handstand, heels tapping lightly against the wall until he got his balance. Under her astounded gaze he slowly bent his elbows to lower himself headfirst toward the floor, then raised back up. "This is harder than it used to be," he said through his teeth.

Shoulder presses. Of course. Afraid she'd disturb his concentration, Julia just watched as he went through a dozen repetitions before dropping his feet back down to the floor.

"So are you going to start contortions now?" she asked.

He grinned. "When you don't have weights, you have to improvise."

"Were you a gymnast or something?"

He snorted. "Nah. I was on the basketball team. We took my college team to the Final Four my junior year."

"Final Four?" she echoed.

"The NCAA tournament?"

She shook her head, mystified.

"It's the college championship basketball tournament. A pretty big deal in the sports world. Remember all the sheets with brackets people were passing around the office in March?"

"Vaguely." She pursed her lips and crossed her arms. "I also remember a couple of weekends you were pretty scarce, now that you mention it."

He gave her a delighted grin. "Why Julia, and here I didn't think you cared."

She felt her face heat. "So why didn't you wind up in the NBA and out of my hair if you were a basketball star?"

"I was too short."

"How tall are you, six foot?"

"Six-four."

"And that's too short?"

"For the NBA." He gave her a wolfish look. "For other things, I'm just right."

In his tropical-patterned boxers and bare feet, he

looked like a beach boy who'd lost his way. His skin gleamed with a faint sheen of sweat. He looked just right.

And she did her damnedest to remember why it was that he just wasn't right for her.

12

PAPER TOWELS, ALEX DISCOVERED, were not the best for drying off after a shower. "Note to the conservation lab staff," he announced, walking out to the lab carrying his T-shirt in one hand, picking off bits of paper towel lint with the other. "If you're going to have a shower, you should at least provide towels."

"I don't think they planned it as a locker-room shower. It's the one you're supposed to run to if you accidentally douse yourself in hydrochloric acid or something."

"Ah. That's why you turn it on by pulling the big ring on the chain."

She nodded. "And why it has no shower curtain."

"Can I help it if I needed to clean up?"

"That was because you insisted on getting all hot and sweaty."

He smiled, then slipped on his T-shirt, covering up the display of washboard abs, she noticed, relieved.

She sniffed and turned to get some more coffee. "While you were making yourself beautiful, some of us were working."

"And here I was hoping you'd be watching."

"Sorry to disappoint you." She threw him a glance over her shoulder while she was still pouring.

It was a fatal mistake.

A splash of hot coffee dripped on the fingers holding the mug. She jerked her hand reflexively out of the way, dropping the mug the three inches to the counter and sending a gout of liquid splashing up.

And cascading over the front of her before she could move.

"Dammit!" The coffee dripped down her skirt, even as she snatched up paper towels. She mopped herself, but not in time to eliminate the wide, dark stain that spread out on the silk. "It's brand-new," she wailed. "I loved this suit."

"Well, it's not new anymore." Alex's voice was dry. "Between being worn for twenty-four hours straight and being dripped on, I'd say it has a trip to the dry cleaners coming."

Her mouth twisted with disgust. "Are you kidding? Coffee stains fabric unless you get it out immediately. In five minutes this suit will be toast." She didn't add that it was couture, with a price tag approaching the cost of a small car. She didn't consider herself one of the frivolous ones who bought a new couture gown for every gala and discarded it after a single wearing. She did, however, believe in paying for quality when it came to classic clothing that, if carefully tended, would wear for years.

Julia didn't think pouring coffee down the front of herself counted as careful tending. Dispirited, she dabbed at the patches of wet—and now cold and clammy—fabric. Great. She'd ruined her suit, her skirt was all wet and she now smelled of eau de java.

And there was still no sign they were ever going to get out of the lab.

Something gray dangled before her. She glanced up to see Alex holding out his shirt. "I know it's got a little mileage on it," he said hastily, forestalling her protest.

"It does have the virtue of not being soaked with coffee, though. It's got to be more comfortable than what you're wearing's going to be." He glanced over at the rack of lab coats that hung by the door. "I mean, you could put on one of those, but at least I can vouch for this one. It's been tenderly worn. Spent the day in air-conditioning. It's a Hugo Boss," he wheedled, holding it out.

She worked her lips and finally surrendered to the smile. "Give me that." She swiped it from his hand. "I'll be in the shower if you need me."

Being clean, she discovered, however minimally, improved her outlook dramatically. Leaving the skirt to soak in a sink full of cold water, she finished drying off and slipped her arms into Alex's shirt.

It smelled like him.

Not like guy, I've-been-in-this-all-day smell. Thanks to the air-conditioning, she couldn't catch a hint of that. What she could smell, though, was the scent of his aftershave, his deodorant, lingering around her. Wearing his shirt was like having his arms around her. Her knees went weak.

ONE BENEFIT TO BEING head conservator, Alex thought as he sat at Wingate's desk, was having the most comfortable chair in the place. He leaned back to put his feet up, but his toes came too close to the wooden box with the statue. Julia would not be amused if he knocked it off and broke the damned thing, Alex decided, sitting upright. And it was a statue worth keeping.

Flipping the clasp free, he opened the lid and stared down at the impassive stone figure. So crude and yet there was something inifinitely more compelling about it than some pretty French ceramic. He hadn't told Julia the entire truth about coming to New

York. Part of it was for the challenge, sure, but part of it was that he loved the ancient things just as much as she did.

Alex took a final look and reluctantly closed the box. Julia, he was sure, would lecture him about exposing the statue unnecessarily to light and air. Better to entertain himself some other way, he thought, glancing around the office.

"I'm back," Julia announced, and Alex glanced up from skimming through one of Paul's books.

For a moment, he was afraid his heart had quite simply stopped. How was it that the same garment could look so astoundingly different on a female-type person? The vee of the neckline, sweeping down to the first closed button made him very aware of the soft, pale skin of her throat and the very intriguing curves below. Even folded up, the sleeves bumped her forearms. A length of cord secured the shirt around her waist. The tails hung down at the front and back to about the length of a short—very short—miniskirt, exposing an eye-popping length of long, lovely thighs. From the side where the hem cut up, well, it was downright scandalous.

She looked as if she'd just climbed out of bed and pulled on one of his shirts for temporary covering before she got in.

"What do you think?" she asked.

That he'd been out of his mind to give her the shirt so he'd have to watch her walk around looking like that? That he had no idea how he was going to keep his hands off her for two days? It took him two tries to speak. "I think you could sell a lot of shirts for Hugo Boss." He cleared his throat. "How's your skirt?"

"Oh, I put it in to soak for a bit. The stains might not come out—it might ruin the fabric, for that matter—but at least I've tried." She glanced at the book in his hands. *"Conservation in Ancient Egyptian Collections?"* she read.

"I'm learning how to get grime and wax out from between the toes of statues."

"Well, that sounds exciting."

Not nearly as much as looking at her, he thought. "Well, I take my entertainment where I can find it. Felix likes to sleep in on the weekends."

"I don't suppose you want to do some more research," she asked casually, picking up her temporarily abandoned coffee mug.

"Don't spill coffee on that," he warned her. "I'm running out of clothes for you. Though you might look kind of fetching in my suit coat, now that I think about it." She might look fetching in anything, he thought feverishly, watching her as she leaned against the counter, slender and leggy and altogether delectable.

"I found a chronology of the abbey earlier, while you were showering," she said.

The words didn't register right away, probably because his synapses had been singed. "The abbey," he repeated blankly and then stared at her attentively. "You mean *the* abbey?"

"'Blessed by a man of God,' the woman said. What's a better source for men of God than an abbey two miles away?" She turned toward the book room and he followed her like a man hypnotized.

The door of the book repository hissed as she opened it. She didn't look any less tempting in the dry, sedate surroundings of the book room. Then again, he couldn't think of any surroundings where she would. "So you found a historical review?" he asked, doing his damnedest to get his brain working again.

Julia's eyes gleamed. "Better. It's their own living history, pretty much a week-by-week diary."

Just then, being a celibate monk was the last thing he could imagine. "How long does it run?"

"It looks like it starts in the late twelfth century. It goes on for a hundred years, maybe more. I didn't go through the entries for all of them." She pointed to the shelves. "Have you ever seen anything like it?"

It was like some sort of surreal medieval encyclopedia, ponderous leather-bound volumes filling an entire bookcase, the gold-leafed inscriptions on their spines worn but still faintly gleaming even after centuries worth of handling.

Still… Alex turned to her. "You realize it'll take weeks, maybe even months, to get through all these." Not that sitting by her side for weeks and months didn't have its appeal.

"That's the thing—we don't have to get through all of them," she told him, eyes glimmering with excitement. "The museum went through a big indexing project in the early nineties, detailed the contents of a lot of the volumes and scrolls. It should give us at least some idea of what's there."

She sat down at the computer and began clicking keys. "See? It goes from 1190 to almost 1500. No wonder there are so many volumes."

"Seems like kind of a strange holding for a museum of antiquities."

"It says here it was part of a bequest from the Toupin family. When you're a not-for-profit, you never say no, you know that. Anyway, they were French. Who knows, maybe they're our manor family. We didn't get all the volumes, but we have most of them." She studied the screen.

And he studied her.

"Oh, this'll work," she said. "They took an inventory of the entire abbey in 1346."

"Interesting timing," he remarked, focusing his attention on the screen for the first time.

"How so?"

"That would have been in the middle of the Hundred Years War."

"Would they have been caught up in it?"

Alex considered. "Could be. They were close enough to Calais and Crécy to see their share of trouble. In theory, an abbey would be immune from the fighting, but when men are in the field, far from their command, you never know."

"Let's take a look." She headed over to the stacks. "Was there a lot of skirmishing in the war?"

"Depends what part you're looking at." As everything did, he thought, watching the sway of her hips as he followed her to the shelf. "The English held Calais for almost two centuries and ran sorties from it. Crécy was even closer. It's entirely possible the abbey could have been threatened." He took the heavy book she pulled from the shelf and carried it back to the tables.

They settled down, side by side. Her scent had lessened in the night, but it was still there, a scent that meant Julia to him, subtle and complex.

As she opened the book, he leaned closer to see the page.

And inhaled surreptitiously.

"Oh, hell." Julia stared at the vellum. "The index didn't mention it was written in French."

"What did you expect? It was a French abbey."

"They were Catholic monks."

"And nuns," Alex interjected, glancing down the printed contents sheet that she'd set aside.

"Either way, they're supposed to write in Latin," she said impatiently.

"It was a daily journal, one more hassle for them. They used whatever language came most easily to the writer—French for some, Latin for others. Just not this one."

"They should have done all of their writing in Latin." Frustration bubbled in her voice. "Latin, I know. Greek, I know."

"Never bothered to learn French, did we?"

She shot him a narrow-eyed look. "If I'd specialized in European art, I'd have learned French. I specialized in antiquities."

"So you learned to speak the language of dead people."

"Funny."

Alex shifted the book to leaf through the pages of beautifully inscribed vellum. "So how much is it worth to you to know what's on these pages?"

Julia gave him a suspicious look. "Why do I get the feeling I'm about to be scammed?"

"Not at all. It just so happens that in addition to my many other talents, I speak French."

"You speak French." She eyed him.

"Three years in high school, three in college. What can I say? I really wanted that semester abroad in Paris so I could learn to pick up French chicks."

"That doesn't surprise me even a little."

He grinned. "You could at least be impressed by my planning, *mon petit chou.*"

"Mon petit chou?"

"My little cabbage. A French endearment."

"You silver-tongued devil, you."

"I admit, I'm a little rusty in conversation, but I'm still pretty good on paper. Let me at this bad boy." He pulled the book closer and tried to concentrate on the pages and not her legs, shown off so nicely by his shirt. Lucky damned shirt, to be wrapped all around her. "I'll read you the intro and then we can go through the pages together. White Star translates as *étoile blanche*, by the way."

"How do you say *ivory?*"

"Haven't a clue." He brightened. "But I know six different ways of cussing a person out."

"Nice to see you spent your semester abroad constructively."

"I also learned some great French pickup lines."

"I'm sure you did. *Mon petit chou.*"

"Didn't I tell you you were getting a soft spot for me?"

Julia shook her head. "Read, please."

"Okay." Amused, he scanned the page. "Let's see. It was a double abbey, like we said, which could have made for some interesting parties."

"Oh yeah, you know those wild monks. I expect they locked the women behind gates."

"Oh, not entirely," he told her. "You're going to love this. Apparently the chicks ran the show."

"Beg pardon?"

"The abbey was presided over by an abbess, not an abbot. Pretty common, from what I recall. They might not have let them preach or hear confession, but they knew that no one can kick butt like a nun."

A corner of her mouth twitched. "You know this from personal experience?"

"Sadly. I went to St. Mary's parochial school up through sixth grade." He rubbed his knuckles absently.

"So that stuff with the rulers and the knuckles isn't a joke?"

"No joke."

"Here I would have figured a slick guy like you

would give them that innocent smile and just slide out of any trouble around."

"Who says I ever did anything wrong?" He gave her his best innocent stare, the one that had worked on all the nuns.

But not, apparently, on Julia. "Ever got caught, you mean."

"I was a model student in all ways."

"I'm just sure you were. Read the account, please."

He grinned and went back to scanning the page. "It looks like the fighting came right up to their doorstep."

"That must have been a shock."

"Listen to this. 'This morning, an engagement took place in the copse below the front portal. We attempted to provide such aid to the fallen, of both camps, as we could, all men being equal in the eyes of God. Frère William sustained an injury from an arrow, though 'tis slight and did not keep him from his evening devotions.

"'The abbess fears that we shall perhaps be overrun if the exigencies of battle force it, for war is a capricious force of destruction before which none are safe. Accordingly, she has ordered an inventory of the abbey's possessions, and that they shall be hidden away, buried in the deepest cellars until this conflict be safely behind us.'" He glanced at Julia. "I wonder what she'd have said if someone told her it was going to last a hundred years. More than."

"How can people spend a hundred years fighting over someone else's land?" She shook her head. "How can you spend that much time killing?"

"They were far less efficient at it than they are now," he said drily.

"Did it ever depress you, studying all of this? I mean, isn't that most of what history is—one war after another, with occasional intermissions?"

"There's more. Watching the world change over time. The majority of people today live better, longer. And for every idiot ruler who starts a war, there are people like Frère William, going out onto a battlefield to help, even though it would have been easier and safer to hide away. That's what history is about, people like him."

"That's an optimist's view."

"I'm nothing if not an optimist," he said softly, giving in to temptation, finally, and reaching out to brush a strand of hair out of her eyes.

She didn't move away, as he'd expected. Instead she studied him. "Why didn't you ever teach?"

"Like my parents?"

"Why not? You said you admired them. And you've got a subject here you really love. Why not do something with it?"

"I *do* do something with it. I work on behalf of the museum."

"Sure, taking people out to lunch and dinner and pumping them for money."

"To keep this museum running." Even he could hear the edge in his voice. "Allowing people like you and Paul to preserve things so that some little girl someday can walk in and see a cup and get an inkling of how she fits into the world."

The rebuke came out sharper than he'd intended. Julia just stared at him, gaze unnervingly steady, as though she were studying something entirely new. He drummed his fingers on the tabletop, suddenly irritated at having been held to account—again. "Hey, well, we should look through this inventory list."

"Maybe we should," she said quietly.

Columns of items covered the open sheets of vellum, some entries filled in with brief details of value, provenance, age. There were pages of it, he realized. "We're going to have to work on this together," he said. "Move in close and we can each take a side of the page. Scan for the words *blanche* or *étoile.*"

Silence filled the room. Silence worked for him. He wasn't all that sure he wanted to have any more conversation just then. He wasn't at all sure he'd like the direction it had been going.

Julia turned to him. "A little free-flowing anxiety?"

"What?" He looked to where she pointed, realized he'd been rapidly bouncing his leg. "Oh, sorry." He stilled it.

The quiet returned, except for the turning of the pages. Julia stirred. "Here?" She pointed to some words.

Alex read them. "*Chandelle blanche.* Uh, no, that's white candle."

"Oh. Well, it was the word *blanche.*"

"Ten points for effort."

They lapsed into silence again, broken only by the sound of their breathing.

"What about that?" Julia asked.

This time he looked at her. "White cup."

"Sorry," she said insincerely, a grin hovering beneath.

He felt his frustration ease and noticed that they were breathing in sync, that her hand had slipped over the arm of her chair to brush unconsciously against his. And it brought not the usual sizzling awareness, but a quiet connection different than anything he'd felt with her before.

And it was because they were connected that he felt it when she tensed. "Alex, what about this?" Her voice vibrated with urgency. No teasing this time, this was for real.

He scanned the page and felt the hairs prickle on the back of his neck. "Ladies and gentlemen, I think we have a winner, brought to us by the lovely Julia Covington. Wave to the crowd, Ms. Covington." Julia gave a little float-lady wave. "Okay, Ms. Covington, let's see what we've got."

13

"READ IT," JULIA BEGGED Alex. "I'm dying here."

"Give me a sec. It doesn't come as quickly as it used to." He cleared his throat. "Lessee…it says, 'One amulet, provenance unknown, fashioned of—' *ivoire,* it says, which I assume is ivory—'in the shape of a star with five points. It shows two tiny dots of carnelian on the front and is but finely cracked along the back.'"

Julia clutched at Alex's shoulder. "Alex, the crack."

"I know."

She nudged him. "Keep going."

"'We know not how this thing came to be in our care. It is clearly pagan, but many pagan things have been won over through prayer, and it appears thus with the amulet. Frère Joseph, our librarian, insists a verse from the Roman poet Adeodatus describes this object, down to the faint carvings on the front that can be discerned by only the sharpest eyes (the author, alas, not being in possession of such, must take them only by report).

"'The words of Adeodatus tell of a desert kingdom and the purest of loves and a White Star that brings that love to those whose hearts remain unsullied. Pagan nonsense, withal, but if a Roman truly wrote about this amulet, then it must be very ancient indeed.'"

"Unsullied hearts," Julia repeated. "Pure of heart. It comes up over and over."

"It's a pretty strong concept," Alex observed. "Purity was much more fashionable in historic times than it is these days."

"I don't think true love ever goes out of fashion," she argued. "It's what everyone truly wants, deep down inside, isn't it?"

"What, true love?" A corner of his mouth quirked.

"Yes," she snapped, rising to the bait. "A soul mate. Someone you connect with so much that it's about way more than sex, it's about who you are. Don't tell me that you don't want that. Everybody wants that. It's like finding your place." She took a breath. "Finding your forever-and-always true love…" She trailed off, staring at him.

Alex looked back at her, his eyes unfathomably dark and deep. The moment stretched out, endless and lost in place and time, as the whole room around them faded into nothingness. His deep green gaze was everything, holding her, pulling her, drawing her until she felt herself tipping, tilting, falling into those deep green pools, falling into him.

Then her elbow slipped off the arm of the chair. She started, yanked abruptly out of the moment.

Swallowing, she gave herself a brisk shake. "Anyway, is there any more there?"

Alex took a moment to answer. "No." He glanced at the page. "That's the end of the entry. Do we have any translations of Adeodatus here?"

"I can't think why we'd have any poetry, but I'll check." Julia turned to the computer, relieved to have something to do.

"Do you know anything about him?"

"Adeodatus?" Her fingers flew over the keys. "Not really. He was Roman?"

Alex nodded. "He specialized in love poems. It makes perfect sense that he would have written about the White Star."

"But how did he stumble across it?" *Think about the research,* she reminded herself. *Don't think about that moment, that sense of being balanced on the edge of a very great fall. And don't, absolutely don't, think about Alex.* "There's no way we're going to find out anything with our resources," she said, frowning at the screen. "We don't have Adeodatus or even any poetry anthologies or resources. And there's no telling what his source could have been. He could have heard it from a traveler—"

"Or stopped in at the library of Alexandria—"

"Or maybe it was a legend that was already so widely circulated that everyone just knew it."

"Collective mythology?"

"Sure." And as she applied herself to the intellectual exercise, she began to relax. Living in her mind was always safest. It was living in her heart that she mistrusted. "How many of the ancient myths are shared among cultures? Wars, invasions, the capture of slaves. People traded gods around like baseball cards. The Romans added the gods of half the countries they invaded. This could have been like that, traveling from country to country until people had no idea where it started."

"You mean like 'Once upon a time, in a kingdom far away…'"

"Exactly."

"Once upon a time, in a kingdom far away lived a prince who was cruelly imprisoned in a conservation lab, though he had done no wrong. And lo, through the days and the nights he suffered privation and hunger and translated French and longed for a princess to offer him succor and mop his brow and feed him Twix bars."

Julia's lips twitched. "Twix bars, huh?"

"If we have any more. If not, I'll take mummy flesh."

"You *are* hard up, my poor prince."

Alex rose. "Somehow I'm detecting a distinct lack of sympathy."

"Oh, *mon petit chou,* no. I'm all over sympathy for you." She stood and felt the whisk of air under her…well, it couldn't properly be called a dress, certainly. Not even a mock dress, not with all the leg it showed. And Alex was definitely aware of it, she thought, catching his glance as they made their way out to the main lab, where they'd piled their booty. "Here," she said to distract them both, "have a Snickers."

"I don't want a Snickers."

"A granola bar?"

He pushed out his lip. "I don't want a granola bar."

"Cheese crackers?"

"There has to be something else in this office."

"You're not going to find a burger and a beer, I'll clue you in."

He started across the lab. "We haven't checked Paul's desk yet."

"I'm not sure we should." Julia's voice was uneasy.

"Why not? We've checked everywhere else, and in case you haven't noticed, we're down to our last few Milky Ways."

"But he's the head conservationist."

"Then he probably has well-preserved food. I think it'll be okay, and if he gets upset about it, he can talk to me." Alex stopped and gave her an appreciative look. "Better yet, he can talk to you. If he sees you in that outfit, he'll give you whatever you want."

"You're funny."

"You're the one who said you were in love with him this morning."

"Pure love, remember? Platonic?"

He looked at her. "Not true love?"

She reddened and looked away.

Alex stepped into the office and flipped on the light. "You said Paul works weird hours, right?"

"Yeah."

"So he probably keeps something here." He began searching the desk. "He has a coffeemaker. Who knows, maybe we'll get lucky and find some Cup-a-Soup." He rifled through the top drawer, "Or maybe an—oh, baby, come to *papa.*"

"What did you find? A ham sandwich?"

"Better." He stared at the plastic wafer feeling something very close to love.

"What's that?"

He turned to the desk and pulled the laptop toward him. "That, my dear, is a Wi-Fi card."

"Wi-Fi?"

"A wireless network card to get Internet service in airports and cafés. Places like that. He probably uses it on travel." Alex slid the card into its slot with a snap, with only an inch or so projecting beyond the computer case.

"You didn't get it put in all the way," Julia told him.

Alex pushed on it a little. "It's supposed to stick out like that. That must be why he had it tossed in his desk. A decent laptop would already have the antenna installed." Life in the nonprofit environment meant that you made do. Then again, a laptop was a laptop. Alex pulled the computer closer and began nosing around the Start menu. "The thing is, if there's an open network around here, we might be able to get online. We can't send messages on his mail application or people won't know it's us, but we can go to a Web-mail site and set up an account." He brought up a window listing local wireless connections. "Okay, do you feel lucky?"

Julia scanned the little window. "They're all pass-word-protected."

"Nearly all. But look at this sweet thing."

"Netgear, unsecured network," she said slowly.

"Exactly. Let's hope it's a home network or that somebody's working Saturdays."

They stared at the screen as the tiny icon of the antenna sent out little dots. Suddenly, it disappeared and a tiny image of a computer sprang up, showing the connection.

"That's it, we're on!" Julia was jubilant. "Go to the Net. Forget about Web mail, just go to the NYPD site. I'm sure they've got a way you can mail them directly. Open up the browser."

And Alex just sat, staring at the screen.

"Alex, open up the browser." She looked at him. "What's wrong?"

What was wrong was that if they sent e-mail to enough people, they would be rescued. It was a given. He should have been happy about it. He was starving. Being locked up was driving him crazy.

Being with Julia felt just right.

He needed more time, he thought. He was making progress. They were connecting—the moment in the book repository had demonstrated that to him. But he needed more time to change her mind, to show her what they could be together. He needed more time to convince her to give them a chance.

Turning away wasn't an option, though. It wasn't just his choice, his life. He owed it to her to do whatever possible to get her out.

Alex stirred. "Okay, let's get this show goin...*dammit to hell.*"

They both saw the red line appear across the wireless-network icon at the same time.

Connection broken.

"Bring it back up," Julia said urgently. "Click on it."

But when he brought the connections page back up, the network didn't show.

"What's happened to it?"

"Who knows? A glitch maybe. Or maybe the server or the broadcast unit has been turned off altogether." He glanced at his watch. "It's twelve-thirty. Maybe whoever was working this weekend has gone home."

"So that's it? It's just gone? Check again," she demanded. "It could have come back."

It hadn't, though, nor had it five minutes later. Or ten. Or fifteen.

"We can keep checking," Alex said, "but we might as well give it up for now." He gave her a level look. "We can't get out."

"I can't believe this," Julia fumed, staring at the screen as though the power of vision would make the network reappear. Then she blinked and leaned forward. "Huh. Well, that's weird."

Alex followed her gaze. "What are you looking at?"

"The e-mail messages that came in while we were connected. The top one, the one from Egypt. It's..." She frowned at the preview pane.

"Full sentences, Julia. Help me out here."

"Oh. Never mind," she said dismissively. "It's just spam. I got confused for a second—his e-mail looks different from mine. The message is from sphinxnet, and there's an antiquities dealer in Cairo who's known as 'the Sphinx.'"

"So?"

"He's reputed to have a somewhat…flexible code of ethics."

"Meaning he deals in stolen goods?"

"Meaning he deals in anything at all if the price is right."

Alex flicked a glance at the screen. "Well, considering the subject line is Hot and Horny Teens, I'm thinking you're right about the spam. Unless they're talking about museum-quality implants."

"You're a regular laugh riot."

"Well, speaking of spam, we came in here looking for food. Let's find some."

"We should really shut down his computer, Alex, or at least close down his e-mail."

"Conscience getting you?"

"It's private. How would you like someone reading your messages? You should close it down."

"No way. If that network comes back up, I don't want to miss it. I'll turn up the volume nice and loud." He fiddled with some menus and suddenly the computer emitted the loud ring of an old-fashioned telephone. "There. That's what we'll hear anytime a new message comes in. You hear that ring, get that delicious fanny of yours in here because it means we're back online. Now, about that food…"

ALLARD WALKED ALONG the low stone wall of Battery Park, looking out at the Hudson River beyond. He stared at the cell phone in his hand. Secure, they'd assured him, an automatic link to the man he was working for. He'd tried without success to get it to display the number it was calling, but then it was unlikely that whatever number it was calling was in any way traceable to his very elusive client.

So he pressed the Send button and listened to it ring in his ear as another phone was ringing on a faraway continent.

"Allô?"

"You know who this is," Allard said. There were few in the world who could call Henri Renouf. A more foolish man would, perhaps, be flattered. Allard was not. It did not matter to him that Renouf could have bought any building on the Champs Elysées thrice over. It did not matter to him that Renouf could force almost any owner to sell. All that mattered was that Renouf was a customer and Jean had the product. The only product. And if Renouf was not willing to buy, Jean could find another buyer.

There was only one White Star.

"Yes, I know who this is." Renouf's voice was cold, emotionless, the voice of a reptile. "What I do not know is why you are not even now before me, completing your task."

"There have been…complications," Allard replied.

"You were recommended to me as a master of your craft. You were brought in expressly so there would be no complications."

"You did not tell me when you hired me that the prize was so coveted," Allard said silkily. "I have come to understand more since. Much more."

"You were told what you needed to know to accomplish your job."

"And I accomplished it."

"Did you? Do I see you here now? Do I hold it in my hand? I grow impatient."

"Perhaps if you showed more gratitude, *monsieur.*" Allard's voice turned hard, like the iron of the ornate black benches he passed.

"More gratitude?" The words were icy.

"We both know the price is inadequate." Allard watched two gulls battle over the same piece of fish, fighting and tearing at it with their sharp beaks. "This prize is worth far more than the pitiful sum you offered."

"You forget yourself."

"I am not the one with the empty hands, *monsieur*. There are always other buyers, but there is only one of what you seek."

"What do you want?" Renouf asked, grinding out the words.

Allard thought of the feel of the ivory in his hand. How very little he wanted to give her up. It would take money, a great deal of it, to ease the hold she had on his mind. "Double the fee."

"You are mad."

"Very well, *monsieur*. *Au revoi*—"

"Wait." The word almost leaped out of the phone.

Allard smiled slowly. *"Oui?"*

There was a long moment of silence. Allard watched a ferry chug its way to Staten Island. "One and a half times the fee," Renouf said finally.

It only amused him. Such a weak attempt, an admission that Renouf would do what was necessary. An admission that Renouf wanted. "I do not negotiate, *monsieur*. If you do not want it, very well. Someone else will."

"Be careful. It is a foolish man who is overconfident."

"Why should I not be confident? I control the prize, do I not? Our feet do not even stand on the same continent."

"There are airplanes."

"Indeed, *monsieur*, there are. Coming and going."

Renouf blew out a breath. *"D'accord.* You will have your money."

And Allard felt the surge of triumph. He smiled broadly. "Very well. When the bank in Switzerland confirms the deposit, I will deliver it."

"In person."

"But of course, *monsieur.* And until then, I will keep her very, very safe."

"If it is harmed in any way, your life will become unpleasant in ways you cannot imagine."

"She will be treated with only the utmost tenderness."

"There have been those who have attempted to trifle with me in the past," Renouf said thinly. "They did not fare well. You may wish to keep that in mind."

Something in the words raised the hackles on the back of his neck. Empty threats, he reminded himself. "*Monsieur,* I have only the greatest respect for you."

"You will find the money in your account Monday. I will expect you then."

"And both of us will be the happier, *monsieur. Au revoir.*" Before Renouf could respond, Allard hung up. Staring out at the water, he chuckled in satisfaction. Two million euros. Two million. A man could live like a king on such a sum. Extravagant wines. Lavish meals. And women, the women he would have.

Starting now.

HE SAT, MOTIONLESS, his knuckles still clenched tightly around the telephone receiver. Beyond the windows lay the blue of the French Mediterranean. Finally, he rose and walked through the glass door and onto the deck, crossing to the railing that overlooked the rocks and the seething ocean below.

The setting sun sent shadows slanting across the cedar. Dragonflies whisked around in the light offshore breeze, hovering on the fragile transparent traceries of their wings. The cries of seabirds sounded far below. The air smelled of salt water.

All his, the lavish villa, the white yacht bobbing at anchor, the rugged coastline, the sea view beyond.

And the White Star.

Like a flash, his hand snapped out and snatched one of the dragonflies out of midair. For a moment he caged it loosely, savoring its frantic fluttering, feeling the soft brush of it against his palm. Then his fingers closed on it convulsively, crushing the wings. He made no sound. Nothing in his expression changed.

Almost as an afterthought, he opened his hand and tilted it over, sending the crumpled remains of the lace wings tumbling down to the foaming sea below.

He turned to the two hard-faced men who'd followed him outside. "Find him. Take the amulet." He dusted off his hands. "And kill him."

14

"I'M BEGINNING TO FIND your compulsions fascinating." Julia leaned back in one of the wheeled chairs in the main laboratory, watching Alex kick around a wad of paper and tape as though it were a soccer ball. As incongruous as he appeared in dress slacks and T-shirt, he still moved with the economical grace of an athlete. There was an energy about him that made it impossible for her to look away.

His motions were practiced, natural. If he'd been in the outside world, it was entirely possible he'd be doing it with a real ball. He might belong to a league, even. She didn't know how he spent his days, she realized; she'd only been a part of his nights.

"So what do you do with your weekends in the outside world?" she asked, turning herself idly back and forth with one toe.

"Depends on the weather." Alex caught the ball with his foot and did something complicated to redirect it. "Usually, I'll bike or run in the park or hit the gym. I belong to a city-league basketball team, so we have a game on Sunday. Sometimes I take my kid sister to brunch. Catch the Cubs game if I can. You know, hang." He glanced up. "How about you?"

"It depends on the weather. If it's nice, I'll walk in the park or take a drive up the Hudson or into Connecticut to go antiquing. Sometimes I'll go to an estate sale. Catch a movie, or read, relax." She smiled briefly. "You know, hang."

He missed the ball and it rolled under the table with the mummy. "See? Perfect match. We're meant for each other." He ducked under the table to retrieve the ball and then straightened, standing by the table. "What's that?" he asked, looking down, and appeared to listen for a moment. "Oh, right, okay." He looked up at Julia. "Felix thinks so, too."

She looked askance at him. "You want me to take dating advice from a thirty-five-hundred-year-old mummy?"

"Hey, have some respect. Felix has been around a while. He knows a thing or two."

"I'm not sure I want to go there," Julia said, rising. When she saw the flicker of desire in Alex's eyes, it brought a flush to her cheeks. She smoothed down the tails of the shirt, feeling the warmth of her palms through the fabric.

"It doesn't work," Alex said. "I can't not see you, Julia, and you can't not see me."

"I can go concentrate on something else, though," she said firmly and headed for the book repository.

"Really? What are you going to work on?"

"The chronicles."

"Planning to pick up a little French, are we?"

She gave him the countess look. "They're not all in French, remember? Besides, when I get to the French parts, all I have to do is look for the word *white* and bring it to my translator." She stopped, with her hand on the door to the book repository. "Assuming you're still willing."

"I don't know, what's in it for me?" Alex asked, bouncing the wad of paper from foot to foot, then kicking it up and into his hands.

"Angling for my share of Paul's protein bars?"

"I was hoping for a more concrete demonstration of your appreciation."

She leaned against the doorway. "My, my, my, hope springs eternal, doesn't it?"

"I could do some more pull-ups, if that'll inspire you," he offered.

Julia eyed him. "How about if you just put it on my tab?"

THE SOUND OF Miles Davis's mournful trumpet played quietly in the room, drifting out of Alex's cell-phone jukebox. Julia scanned the printed summary page that had been tucked into the front of the volume of the chronology she was working on. Next to her, Alex bent over a book of his own.

The song ended and he picked up the phone, fiddled with it and set it back down. After a moment, "Strangers in the Night" flowed out into the room.

Julia raised her eyebrows. "Frank Sinatra?"

"It's the last of the slow stuff. After that we're on to Green Day and Franz Ferdinand."

"Nice to know you've got eclectic tastes."

"In music. In women, I'm much more single-minded."

His gaze made her warm, and very conscious of the fact that his shirt did little to cover her legs when she was sitting. "Yes, well, focus is important."

His teeth gleamed. "That's what I always say."

Julia paged through the volume she was working on—Latin, mercifully—searching for mentions of the White Star. They'd stumbled over the book in the inventory, finding out where the amulet was. Now, she was mostly finding out where it wasn't.

Frank Sinatra sang about doing it his way as she worked her way through the year 1282, reading of land deals and politics, harvests and storms. Frank gave way to Coldplay then matchbox 20 then P.J. Harvey. Julia stretched her arms lazily into the air, then leaned her head back and rubbed her neck.

Suddenly, Alex straightened. "Julia." Urgency vibrated in his tone.

"Did you find something?"

"Yeah. Yeah, I did."

"When?"

"From 1211. It's written by the abbess of the time. She was the chronicler at this point."

"Another smart woman."

"Can't get enough of them. Pretty sloppy penmanship for a nun, though," he noted. "So, they found one of the sisters with a precious object on her person, which was a pretty big deal given that they took vows of poverty when they joined the order. Not only that, the object was pagan."

"Let me guess, an ivory star that appeared very old."

"Bingo. The abbess took it away from the sister and punished her. Listen to this." Alex scanned the writing until he'd found his spot. "Let's see… 'May the Lord bless Soeur Marie-Thérèse and forgive her her transgressions. For she came to us as a new widow these four years ago, seeking sanctuary. She had no children and wished no part of the material world, but thought to pass her remaining days far from her previous home, quietly, in prayer and contemplation. Her father, Barthélemy, Vicomte de Calfours, made to us a generous gift for her safekeeping, and so all seemed well. She was unfailingly solemn but kind, and devoted herself to the order, relinquishing all worldly things, so we thought.

"'It was thus all the worse to find her with an object so clearly pagan. She appeared at my cell after her punishments, admitting her fault but still desiring its return. She wept piteously, falling to the flagstones before me when I refused.

"'It was her only memento of her husband, Étienne le Brun, baronet and Crusader, she said. They had been but new married when he took the cross and left for the great Crusade, to deliver the Holy Land back unto the Christians. Ah, the Crusade. Many and fearful are the tales we have heard from Constantinople, of the death of Christians by Christians, of fire and chaos.'"

Julia frowned. "Wait a minute. I thought the Crusades were fought over Jerusalem."

Alex gave a humorless laugh. "Toward the end, the Crusades were fought over whatever seemed politically expedient. The Fourth Crusade started out well-intentioned, actually. It only got corrupted later."

"How?"

"Basically, the knights all headed out to Venice, where they were supposed to take boats to the Holy Land. But the Venetians didn't care about high ideals. They were only interested in cash and carry, and the Crusaders didn't have the money."

"So, what happened?" Julia asked.

"The heir to the throne of Byzantium, whose father had been usurped and imprisoned by his brother, offered them a deal—he'd pay for the boats if they'd stop off at Constantinople on their way south and take his throne back for him. He'd get them the money from the treasury once he was restored to power."

"'I will gladly pay you on Tuesday for a hamburger today,'" Julia quoted.

A grin flashed over his face. "You got it. And it went about the way you'd expect."

"So how do you know all this?" And how was it he was talking so casually about obscure historic details, this man she'd always dismissed as an intellectual lightweight?

"I did my senior project on Constantinople and Byzantium, remember?"

"Interesting choice. Why not Greece or Rome or Austria?"

"Why didn't you specialize in Flemish art?" he countered. "Everyone was doing Greece and Rome and Austria. I wanted to do something different. And I wanted a chance to make more of an impact."

"And did you?"

"I aced the class and the project, if that's what you're asking. It was fun. Had me thinking about a graduate degree in history for a while."

"Are you sure you're the Alex Spencer we all know and love?" she said lightly.

His gaze hardened a little. "Maybe that's the Alex Spencer you all seem dead set on having me be."

It felt like a reproach and she lifted her chin. "I see. Well, since you're such an expert, just what did happen in the Fourth Crusade?"

He didn't answer right away. "It wound up getting really ugly," he said finally. "The people of the city didn't want the prince back, but the knights were hell-bent on restoring him to the throne, which made none of them very popular. And, of course, once they did, he didn't have the money to pay anyone."

"Big surprise there," Julia commented.

"Big surprise for the prince. New taxes, lots of

fighting and rabble-rousing. And in the middle of all that, another usuper showed up and deposed him. Then the Crusaders decided to establish discipline and they sacked the city. Easter week, no less. Wound up killing thousands, Muslims, Christians, they didn't care. Burned half the city to the ground and looted what they didn't."

"Great. So Étienne was a looter."

"It was going around."

"Maybe that's why his wife joined the nunnery—to pray for the good of his soul."

"A lifetime of celibacy? Now, that's love." Alex took a drink of water. "Okay, back to the abbess. Étienne went off to the Crusades to loot and pillage, Marie-Thérèse kept the home fires burning. 'Four years passed, during which she prayed morning and night for her husband's safe return, four years with only the fearful tales from Constantinople for comfort. Then one afternoon, even as she settled down for her evening prayers, there was a shout by the front gates. Her Étienne had returned. He was a changed man, though, grim of face and drawn, and so racked with fever he could barely reach his bed.

"'A day passed, then another, and he lingered nigh unto death, saying nothing. And at that final hour, before the arrival of the priest, he pressed upon her an object, the amulet found upon her person.

"'It sits now on my desk and I cannot help but feel a warmth from it. I know it is pagan, but there is a strange beauty to it. It feels not of the devil but of love. Of course, we could not let it remain in the keeping of Soeur Marie-Thérèse, for the good of her soul, but I am curiously reluctant to destroy it. I shall bring it to Frère Michel to do with as he sees fit.'"

Julia turned to Alex. "He brought her the White Star."

"All the way home from Constantinople. A gift from the knight to his lady fair."

"Ironic that he brought back a symbol of purity, considering what the experience had to have done to him. 'Grim of face and drawn.' What do you do when the mob mentality evaporates and you have to live with yourself?" she murmured. "When you have to look into the eyes of the person you love and tell her what you've done?"

"Maybe that was why he didn't."

Julia gave a humorless laugh. "She knew. Why else would she join the convent? She knew and she feared. And when she lost him, she threw the rest of her life into trying to redeem him. It wasn't fair," she burst out. "He owed it to her to be better than that."

Alex gave her a puzzled look. "Owed? You think that's what marriage is about—owing?"

"No, I think marriage—or any relationship—is about trying to bring the best of yourself to the other person," Julia countered. "Trying to always live up to the best within you. Being in love should make you want to do more, be more. And when you're riding in to slaughter and rob innocents, it should be the thing that makes you stop, if nothing else does." The anger evaporated as quickly as it had arrived and she let out a breath. "Sorry, I'm just…" She waved her hands vaguely in the air.

"Don't be sorry," he said, studying her. "I'm learning a lot about you this weekend. I never realized that you felt so strongly about this stuff."

"I'm just talking hypothetically," she said and moved to push her chair back.

"Wait." Alex reached out and with his fingertips turned her to face him. Heat rocketed through her. "So tell me this," he asked. "With all of these very strong ideas about relationships, how is it that you've spent the last six months in a relationship that was almost strictly about sex?"

Because all it took was a look from him to snatch her breath, a brush of his hand to destroy all common sense. Because like Étienne and his Crusade, when Alex Spencer touched her, all her high-minded ideals went by the wayside and she found herself dragged into the rush and heat of something so deeply carnal that she had no control over it. Julia moistened her lips. "I told you, it was a phase. And it's done."

"'Live up to the best within you,' I believe you said?"

Her cheeks heated. "That was just foolish talk." And she needed to stop talking. She needed to focus on the research, focus on the work. *Use your head. Don't think about your heart.* "Okay, we know how the amulet got to the monastery. How do you think it got to the manor house?"

Alex let out a breath. "A land purchase. Or a gift in exchange for protection, maybe. France was in a fair amount of civil turmoil in the sixteenth and seventeenth centuries. Trouble could have landed on the abbey, again."

"It must have been a trade for protection if the manor family held on to it for so long. They had to have done something good to get it."

He gave her an amused look. "Karma, again? Do you really believe that?"

"You've got to admit, it's a pretty interesting series of coincidences," she said, unwilling to be drawn into any more revelations.

"Correlation doesn't equal causation," he reminded her.

"Wow, you really did go to college, didn't you?"

"And so did you."

"I know. But I felt something in that amulet. I can't

describe it. And you said you felt it, too." She locked her eyes on his. "Or was that just a line?"

He held her gaze. "No, it wasn't."

15

Saturday, 8:00 p.m.

WHAT CREEPED HIM out was the dead guys, Fletcher thought as he walked down the hall. He'd done night shift lots of places. It wasn't as if the sound of his footsteps in an empty room spooked him. He'd patrolled offices, warehouses, department stores—even Yankee Stadium on one memorable occasion.

But none of them had been filled with dead bodies. *Old* dead bodies. He was fine with the statues or the sarcophagus things, or even the carved beetles, though why you'd want a three-inch-long jade cockroach he'd never know.

"Christ!" He spun, hand on his stick, heart thudding, scanning the dimly lit room for the face he'd seen. Only to discover one of those spooky-eyed funeral masks staring back at him.

What the hell?

It was all Sherry's fault. She was the one who'd insisted on renting that mummy movie. She thought it was a real hoot. As if the last thing he needed wasn't worrying about the damned things coming to life. Not that he really believed in that kind of stuff or anything, but without a gun on his hip, he was maybe a little jumpy. Hell, what was he going to do if a bad guy—or a mummy—came after him? Pepper spray them to death?

"She-it," he said disgustedly, listening to the echo of his own voice as he stopped at the electronic monitor to punch in his code. At least the next gallery wasn't so bad. The Babylonians and Assyrians didn't wrap people up after they were dead. How twisted was that, for chrissakes? The way he figured it, a man died, leave him in peace. Don't wrap him up and put him on display.

He could just imagine his uncle Louie wrapped up and put on display. Now that would be one big glass case.

He started past the elevator and door to the basement and stopped. Maybe he'd just take a turn around down there, check it out. Nothing wrong with being thorough. He punched the call button to the elevator and with a ping the doors opened.

Hieroglyphs marched around the walls, spacey-looking Egyptian guys in skirts, with that wicked eyeliner. Fashion, he snorted. It had been just as bad then as now. He hit the button for the basement.

The walkie-talkie on his hip buzzed. "Fletcher, what the hell do you think you're doing?"

The elevator began to drop. "Relax, Harry. I'm just getting a change of scenery. What are you doing, getting your jollies watching the elevator cam?"

"I'm not getting my jollies watching you, that's for sure. I don't want you walking out the door into that basement."

"I just wanted to see something different. What's it to you?" The doors folded back, giving him a view of the corridor wall opposite.

"I'll tell you what it is to me, you dipstick. Those monitoring stations are set up so you make your route in a certain time. They see you at one, they expect to see you at the next station in a coupla minutes. You show up late, it prints out on a report. It prints out a report, someone gets mad. And I don't want them smacking me down because I wasn't watching the new guy. You get your ass back up to the first floor, *capisce?*"

Fletcher stared out at the basement hallway with its branching corridors. No mummies, no weird bug carvings. Just plain, peaceful walls. He sighed. *"Capisce."*

JULIA SIGHED AND ROSE. "I need a break before we take this any further. What time is it?" she asked.

Alex gave her an amused look. "You are wearing a watch, you know."

"I know. I just wanted to be sure it's keeping correct time."

"It's a little before eight," he said, following her out into the main lab. "Why?"

"No reason."

But there was a reason, and it became more and more apparent as the minutes passed. She got some water from the tap. She stretched, which made interesting viewing. She took down her hair and ran her fingers through the dark tumble of it, which was also interesting to watch. She put it back up with a practiced swirl.

And she checked her watch. Over and over and over again.

Alex sat backward on a wheeled office chair, his arms resting on the back, watching her. "Are you okay?"

Julia paused in her pacing to glance at him. "Sure. Why wouldn't I be?"

"No reason in particular, except that you've been fidgeting for the past hour. You're going to wear a hole in that floor if you don't watch it."

She reddened. "You play soccer with a taped-up clump of paper, I pace. To each their own."

"Just a guess, but are you maybe a little freaked out at missing your mom's party?"

She snapped her head around to stare at him. "Don't be silly." She resumed walking. "She'll have lots more to worry about than me. It's no big deal."

"Then why are you freaked out?"

"I'm not freaked out, I just—"

"You just what?"

"You don't understand how it is in my family."

"I know when you're a socialite, this kind of thing matters."

"I'm not a socialite," she snapped. "I'm a curator of ancient Egyptian objects."

"And that's part of the problem," he said quietly.

She scowled. "There is no problem. Everything's fine."

"If everything's fine, then why are you logging enough miles for a marathon?" Rising, Alex walked over to stand in front of her, blocking her path. She stopped abruptly, like a startled horse. He'd watched her over the past hours as she'd spun herself up into a minor frenzy over a situation she was powerless to control. He'd watched, staying out of it, saying nothing because he knew she wouldn't want it.

He couldn't sit and watch her anymore. Taking her hands, he raised them to his lips to kiss the knuckles. "Talk to me," he said softly. Julia stared at him, eyes dark. He drew her over to the wooden table to sit. "It's just you and me and Felix in here. Felix won't tell anyone and I won't either," he said, holding on to her hand. "Talk to me?"

She was silent for a long time. "What's your family like?" she asked finally.

"Mine?" The question stopped him for a moment. "I don't know, same as any other, I guess."

"You know there's no such thing."

He'd never really analyzed his family before; they'd simply always been there, solid and dependable. And so he groped for the words. "They're good people. We're there for one another no matter what. If something happened to any one of us tomorrow, the rest of us would show no matter where we had to go, whether we had to get on a bus, a plane, a packet steamer." He smiled crookedly. "Assuming I wasn't locked up here, of course."

"Assuming that. What are your parents like? I know you said they were teachers."

"They're the best," he said simply. "They always wanted us to do well. Not like the pressure to get straight A's and go to Harvard, but somehow the way they encouraged us made us all want to do our best." *To live up to the best within you.* The memory of her words stopped him for a moment. He cleared his throat and went on. "My sister's a lawyer here in New York. She's why I'm here, actually. I wanted to take a chance, take on something more challenging instead of just doing what was easy. Manhattan sounded like a pretty cool place to live, from what she said, so I came here and started from scratch."

"And you've done fabulously, of course."

He shook his head. "You're amazing."

"At what, flattery?"

"No, avoiding talking about yourself." He made an impatient noise. "You do it so smoothly that I don't even notice sometimes."

She tried to tug her hand away, but he held it securely. "Are you saying I'm evasive?"

"I'm saying you're guarded. You're very good at changing the subject, at making plans to go somewhere, at doing almost anything but letting the discussion become personal."

Her cheeks tinted. "So?"

"You're upset about something and you can't do anything about it, which is making you crazy. Why don't you talk to me? Tell me what's going on. I'm not going to be able to change anything, but maybe it will help just to get it out." He gave her a crooked grin. "I told you about my family."

"Mine isn't as warm and fuzzy as yours."

"I'll let that go because I know it's just another way of changing the subject." His gaze was steady on hers. "Come on."

Julia let out a sigh. "The Covingtons have been part of the New York social register for over a hundred and sixty years. There's money, I think you know that, but there are also expectations."

"From your family?"

"From everyone. Maintaining social standing is hard work. There are constant obligations—the parties, the lunches, the committee meetings, the galas. And it bores me silly. I know they raise money, they actually do good works as well as flutter around in couture giving air kisses. I know that I owe my job in part to the fact that I'm on a social basis with a number of our donors."

"You owe your job to the fact that you're good," he countered.

"And the fact that I know people. It still bores me out of my mind. It has from the time I was a kid."

"And they made you go do it all anyway?"

She blew out a breath. "It's not that cut-and-dried. Remember what you said about your parents never forcing you but encouraging you? My mother—Lily—was a little less subtle. The expectation was that I'd do certain things. Lily was deb of the year in 1964. She's headed up the Performing Arts Institute gala for each of the last ten years." Julia turned to him. "That probably doesn't sound like much, but trust me, it's a big deal."

"It's a lot of work, I know."

"I went to cotillion, I had my coming out, and the whole time it all made me crazy."

"What about your aunt Stella? She sounded like she was on your side."

"Stella was great. She thought my mother and aunts were a bunch of ninnies." Julia laughed, the shadows easing for a moment. "She used to say that, literally. 'What is that bunch of ninnies up to now?' She showed me that maybe there was another path."

"Not popular, I take it?"

She furrowed her brow. "I think it confused them more than anything. They didn't understand what I wanted to do and why I wanted to work so hard. That's what Lily always says. 'Why do you want to work so hard?' She's never understood that it's the parties that are the hard work for me."

"Boring?"

"Partly." Julia hesitated. "And partly I'm just shy."

It was a response he'd never have expected. "You, shy?"

"Incredibly."

"But you always look so together, the way you stand there and talk to people. And you've always got a comeback."

She smiled faintly. "Self-defense. If you're shy, that's what you do, find a way to make people laugh."

"But you can think rings around people. I don't get it."

"That's because you're a people person," she said simply. "I'm not. It's an effort for me. And somehow I always wind up carrying the conversation, with everyone looking to me to say something."

She always seemed so cool and confident and in

charge when he saw her at museum functions. It was in-
comprehensible. "So you couldn't tell your mother it
wasn't your thing?"

"I tried. Stella helped. She helped me tell Lily I
wasn't going to Sarah Lawrence. And when Stella put
her foot down, it stayed there." A grin flickered over her
face, quick and private. "She might have weighed a
hundred pounds dripping wet, but she didn't take back
talk from anyone, especially from the daughter of her
ninny of a little sister."

"What's the deal with Sarah Lawrence?"

Julia blew out a breath. "It's the family school. All of
them went there, Lily and my aunt Bitsy, my grandmother. Even Stella went there, at least until she ran off
with the artist. It was the tradition. It was what a nicely
brought up young lady did, and yes, I come from the kind
of family where they still use that kind of language. Not
even my getting into Harvard entirely made it better."

That made him angry on her behalf. "How could
they not be proud of that?"

"You don't understand. I was supposed to go to Sarah
Lawrence and marry the brother of one of my classmates."

It was a different world, one he'd heard about but
never believed in. He hesitated. "I notice you don't
really talk about your dad in all of this."

"Gerald?" Julia snorted. "Gerald ran off with a Dutch
model when I was still in grade school. That was when
Lily changed our name back to Covington."

"She never remarried?"

Julia shook her head. "I think that's why she's so
obsessed with the committee work. It gives her something to fill her life with, especially since my brother and
I grew up. That's what's so hard about this. On one
hand, I'm totally relieved. I'd much rather be trapped

here with you, trading candy bars, than sitting in a swank hall eating a Todd English meal and bidding on couture or whatever they're hawking."

"Thanks. I think."

Amusement flickered for an instant in her eyes, before the unhappiness returned. "But this is her night, her big night. And maybe I think it's criminal that they'll spend three-quarters of what they raise on paying for the party, when they could just write a check straight to the cause, but it doesn't matter. She honestly believes she's doing a good thing. She lives for this."

"We'll get out of here eventually, though. You'll be able to explain."

She studied their clasped hands as though they were something she'd never seen before. "I know, but it's still hard. Things haven't been going so well between us since my divorce, and she's sitting there right now thinking I ditched her. It'll be like a big slap in the face, that I couldn't be bothered to show." Julia blinked and swiped furiously at her eyes. "And she doesn't deserve that. I love her, you know?" She slid off the table and walked a few feet away.

Alex followed her, touched her shoulder. "I know," he said quietly.

"I may not understand her and her life may not make a hell of a lot of sense to me, but I love her. And it kills me to hurt her feelings like this, while she's in the middle of running around trying to make everything perfect for everyone."

He reached out and pulled her to him. At first, she stiffened. "Come on," he murmured, "just relax." And he held her against him.

For the first time in all the many times they'd been together, he touched her with the intention only to comfort.

Desire didn't matter; pulling that miserable look from her eyes did. And when he heard her sigh and felt her soften against him, he bent his head down to kiss her hair.

They had always been about flash and fire, about heat and passion. Now, a quiet warmth simmered between them. Now he wanted only to banish the shadows from her eyes.

Julia sighed, feeling warm and protected in a way she almost never had. She'd opened up to him in a way she rarely did with anyone, and yet somehow she didn't feel vulnerable, she didn't feel exposed. Instead, she felt…reassured, cared for. Comforted. His hand stroked her back. He held her close to the warmth of his body, and in the curve of his arms, she felt safe.

She couldn't have said when it changed, when caring turned to wanting when comfort transformed into the beginnings of need. One moment, she was leaning quietly against him, wanting nothing more than for the moment to stretch out, wanting nothing more than to be held this way forever. The next, desire had flickered to life within her, like the spark that ignites the roaring blaze.

She slid her hand around the nape of his neck and turned her face to his. Surprise. She saw it in his eyes, in the curve of his mouth. She saw the question that she knew only one way of answering.

And she brought his mouth down to hers.

THE ROOM WAS STUFFY and small. Allard ignored it and concentrated on squeezing the bare breasts of the blonde astride him.

"That what you like, baby? Huh?" she grunted, riding him, rising up and down on the cock buried inside her. "You want some more of that?"

"I wish for you to shut up," he said coldly. That was

the benefit of paying for a service. In a restaurant, he ordered what he wished, demanded that everything be to his satisfaction. He would accept no less now. The woman was a paid performer, nothing more. And he would get the performance he desired.

He raised up slightly and pushed her off him. "Suck on me," he ordered, enjoying the quick flash of insult on her face. "Get on your knees." In the lights of the room, he could see the lines on her face that hadn't been apparent outside, could see the stretch marks. She'd been on the street too long and she looked tired, though her mouth was warm and mobile as it slid up and down the hard length of him.

There would be better women soon, though. Young and beautiful, and they'd give him everything he wanted in the villa he'd buy by the sea. Or perhaps there would be a boat, a white yacht he would cruise around the islands, from Capri to Santorini. And servants and hired people to manage all the practical details while he concerned himself only with the pleasure he'd take from the women. Whatever his appetites, he would satisfy them.

"You want to try something else, baby?"

He was getting soft, he realized in annoyance. It was just the useless whore. She did not realize who he was, she did not appreciate what he had done. He fingered the key on a chain around his neck and thought of the White Star, locked up in a box that only he could access.

He felt the throb of his arousal and the whore chuckled and began to speed her motion.

And if he wanted, on Monday he could go to the bank, pull the amulet out of the box, touch her. Have her. She was his for now, lovely and smooth and warm, his alone. For an instant he imagined the feel of her in his hand, imagined possessing her, white and hard and satiny. And his.

And his.

He stiffened and groaned out his climax.

AND JULIA dreamed of the desert...

Warm winds rattled the fronds of the palm trees overhead. She was aware of her body in a way she'd never been in her entire life. And she unfastened her robe and let it drop to the sand, raising her head to meet the green eyes of the man who stood in shadow, watching her.

The press of lips, the heat of mouth against mouth, the brush of hand over skin. The surge of body against body. And in a shimmering moment under the crystalline sky, pleasure exploded into ecstasy.

16

Sunday, May 7, 6:00 a.m.

IT WAS THE LIFE he'd always wanted, the life he'd always deserved, Allard thought: the sun-drenched deck of the white yacht, the sound of the water, the woman working on him with her mouth and her hands while another brushed her enormous breasts against his lips. She moved to straddle him on the chaise—

—and his world exploded into light and white-hot pain.

He came clawing up into consciousness to see the dingy backstreet hotel room in the light of dawn, the bleary-eyed whore beside him.

And the two hard-faced men who stood facing them.

Merde. Allard searched with his tongue for broken teeth. "It is an unkind way to wake a man."

"Our employer is not feeling particularly kind."

The whore began to shriek. Emotionlessly, one of them struck her hard enough to stun her, then tied her stockings around her head in a gag.

Allard struggled to gather his wits. He ignored the clench of fear in his gut. *La Souris Noire,* he heard his father's taunt. But he was not a frightened mouse, he was a professional who had escaped far worse situations than this. He would make the adrenaline work for him. And he was still in control. Consciously, he evened his breathing. Despite their guns, they needed him to get the amulet. He was not expendable.

For now.

He rose from the bed, a spark of insolence in his eyes. "What do you hope to accomplish here? I have the…package and I will deliver it at the appropriate time."

The fist of the taller man lashed out and snapped Allard's head back. Pain exploded through him and he staggered back, knocking over the bedside lamp. Pushing himself upright, he raised the back of one hand to his torn lip.

"You do not speak," the stockier of the two said in an even tone. "The time for speaking is past. Your only task is to do what you are told."

"If your employer wants his prize," Allard began, and another blow sent him down to one knee.

"You do not listen so well, eh? No talk, unless it is to answer questions. We want the package."

"It is not here," Allard said sullenly.

"Then you will take us to it."

"When the money has been transferred, your employer will have his prize." The tall one raised his hand, but Allard only stared back at him belligerently. "I have been beaten before. And a bank becomes suspicious when a bloodied man comes in with others to empty out a safe-deposit box. Tread carefully, my friends. All I want is my money and your employer will have his prize."

The stocky man shook his head. "That is past, now. You have made a very great mistake. There will be no money. You will give us the amulet."

"But I—"

The stocky man moved swiftly to catch Allard by the throat with one hand, hoisting him up until he stood on tiptoe to avoid being throttled. "No *buts*," he hissed. "You are not in control here. Would you like us to demonstrate?"

He released Allard and nodded to the tall man, who dragged the groggy whore to her feet and pulled a silvery bar out of his pocket. With a snick, the bar in his hand became a knife. He turned her away from him, toward the bed.

And with one efficient motion, sliced her throat.

Arterial spray sent a bright arc of scarlet splattering against the far wall as she struggled. Allard felt something hit his face and raised his hands to wipe it off.

They came away red. And staring at the blood, he never saw the blow coming.

When he woke, the angle of the sun had changed only a little. Just a few moments elapsed.

A few crucial moments.

The whore's body was sprawled across the blood-stained bed where they'd thrown it. Next to her, though, was the knife.

"It is a policeman's wet dream," the stocky one said softly. "A murder, a victim, a weapon, complete with fingerprints. Oh yes, there are fingerprints on it," he added as he saw Allard's gaze shoot to their gloved hands. "Yours, my friend. And as you are no doubt aware, any law-enforcement search will bring up your name. Your real name. And they will no doubt find your semen in the condom in the rubbish bin."

He leaned in, gaze flat and hard. "This is all to demonstrate that we mean what we say. We will leave here now and put the privacy sign on the door." He caught up a handful of Allard's hair and pulled his head back. "If you deliver the amulet, we will free you to come back and do what you can to remove the evidence. If not, we will make a phone call to the police and you will

spend the rest of your worthless life in prison." The
stocky one released him. "Now get dressed," he ordered.
"We are leaving."

DARKNESS. THE WARMTH of a body against her, the reassuring rhythm of breath. Julia snuggled closer and sighed.

And then full consciousness hit.

Her first impulse was flight, which was something of
a challenge given that she was locked in, not to mention
curled up in pitch darkness with the very man she
wanted to escape.

Or maybe she wanted to escape her idiotic, impulsive self. Not that she *was* idiotic and impulsive, but
she'd sure been doing a good imitation of it. How the
hell did you have a morning-after experience when
you'd been sleeping with a guy for six months?

She opened her eyes to darkness for the second time
in two days and resisted the urge to groan. She'd
broken up with Alex and been, if not happy with it, at
the very least resigned to the fact that it was the best
thing for both of them. How, then, did she explain the
fact that she'd slept with him again? And it wasn't
something that she could blame on being carried away.
He'd given her the ball and she had—as the saying
went—run with it.

She squeezed her eyes tightly shut until patterns of
red and yellow and orange formed. If she told him that
she still meant it about the breakup and she wanted to
act as if nothing had happened—*Either time?* taunted a
voice in her head—he'd think she was nuts. And right-
fully so. The problem was, she couldn't think straight
when he was touching her. Then again, she couldn't
think straight when he wasn't, clearly, or she'd never
have gone within ten feet of him.

She sighed.

And Alex's arms tightened around her. "You awake?" he murmured.

For a moment, she wanted only to curl up against him and go back to sleep. Instead, she rose and hit the switch, squinting at the flood of brightness. Time to shed a little light on things. "Welcome to my world."

Alex stepped up to her to rest his hands on her hips, smiling. "I kind of like your world," he said. "I kind of like you in mine." He leaned in to kiss her.

And adroitly she ducked away. "You don't happen to have any more of those green strips, do you?" she asked, stepping to the sink. If she let him kiss her, she'd be sunk. She had to stop this, now.

He watched her as though he knew just what she was thinking. "Sure," he said flatly, handing her the package. "Help yourself."

She rinsed her mouth and then put in the breath strip, screwing up her face. "God, I can't wait to use a real toothbrush for a change. And get out of here. We'll be out of each other's hair and be able to breathe."

"I kind of like being locked up with you."

"Alex," she said gently, "this isn't the real world. We're still not right together."

Something very like anger flashed in his eyes. "Oh, last night was just scratching another itch? I thought you wanted something more than just sex."

"I do."

"Then what does it take to convince you? How much more right do you need it to be? Try looking at what's in front of your face instead of what's in your head, Julia. Open up your mind for a change."

"I do have an open mind," she returned, stung.

"You could have fooled me. I'm going to go check

Paul's computer," he said shortly, heading toward the office without turning.

And Julia felt like hell. Okay, so the sex was fabulous. What happened over a weekend of isolation didn't count. They were in a special situation, a situation that wouldn't hold once the door opened. What was she supposed to do, forget the guy she'd known for a year and a half? Forget the man she'd been sleeping with for six months? Was she supposed to believe that he'd suddenly turned into the person she'd been seeing bits of in the past two days? That was just following her emotions and whims, and she'd had enough of that.

She had to take control of her life, she had to start using her head again, not her emotions. Not her heart. She'd already told him where things stood, she knew the right thing to do.

How was it that it didn't feel so right anymore?

ALEX PLUNKED DOWN in the chair at Paul's desk and flipped open the box to stare at the statue of Anibus, fighting back the surge of frustration. Just when he thought he was getting somewhere with Julia, that *they* were getting somewhere, it became very apparent that he really hadn't gotten anywhere at all.

And it bothered him, far more than he'd ever expected it to. Okay, so if he were totally honest with himself, he'd followed her down to the lab two days before partly out of desire, sure, but also partly out of injured pride. Her announcement had shocked him. That wasn't the way it worked in his world. He was the one who walked away from the women. Women weren't the ones who walked away from him, especially not when he was happy with the way things were going.

Especially not when he'd decided he might just want more.

But Julia was so stubborn. Why couldn't she understand that things were different? That he was different—not from who he'd been but from the image she had of him? Something had grown over the time they'd been locked up together, something far stronger and deeper than they'd had before. How could she not see it? How could she block him out and walk away?

And how could he let her?

He shut the top of the artifact box with unnecessary force. The answer was, he couldn't. Not without trying. She might not be ready to admit it, but things between them had shifted already. And the more they were together, the more they would continue to shift. And if that took hanging around and hanging around until she finally acknowledged it, well, that was what he would do.

Because there was no way he was letting Julia Covington walk away.

Feeling better, he tapped the Shift key of the laptop, interrupting the screen saver. The e-mail program still sat open, unchanged; no wireless-network icon showed in the corner. Still, it wouldn't hurt to hang around for a few minutes and see what happened.

Then he looked more closely, puzzled.

With a tap on the door, Julia stuck her head in. "I brought you coffee," she said, holding out a cup.

A peace offering. The mug was too hot to hold, and he set it down. "Thanks."

She perched on the spare chair. "Any luck?" she asked brightly.

Was he surprised that she acted as though nothing had just happened? No.

To keep his hands busy, he picked up one of the books

sitting on the corner of the desk. "Not so far. Looks like our buddy from yesterday decided to stay home."

"Maybe he'll come in later. It's only ten."

"I suppose." Alex glanced down at the book. "*Proceedings of the Fifteenth International Conference on the Conservation of Three-Dimensional Collections, Reims, France, May 2005,*" he read aloud. "No wonder he finds excuses to go to conferences. I'd go to conferences, too, if I could go to Reims in May."

"I hate to break your heart, but he's supposed to leave for this year's meeting this week, I think," she said, pointing to the travel-agency envelope stuck between the jumble of blocks and a box of latex gloves at the back of the desk.

"How do you know that?"

"I'm supposed to leave Tuesday."

Alex shook his head. "I got the wrong job," he muttered. "I go to NEA meetings in D.C. when I could be in Reims learning about—" he thumbed through the book "—formation of calcium oxalate on stone surfaces or microbial species on ecclesiastical polychrome sculptures. Now there's a can't-miss paper. Or, hey, here's one that looks like it gets a lot of mileage, 'The Preparation and Use of Isinglass for Conservation of Polychrome Wood Sculpture.'" He glanced at her. "That's that stuff in the refrigerator, right? He's got a recipe here." He scanned the article and grimaced. "Oh, man, you know this stuff is made by boiling fish bladders? That's disgusting."

"You should smell it cooking."

"I'll pass, thanks."

She gave a half smile. "Well, he'll have to throw it out soon, and you'd better hope you're not around when he does. It's only good for a couple of days. I don't know what he's doing with it."

"Painting the pages of this book, it looks like." Alex turned the page. "He's dripped gunk all over his recipe."

"Well, he'd better watch he doesn't stick the pages together. That's what it's for—adhering things."

"Like dirt?" Alex held up a slip of paper that had been tucked into the book. "And sand and what? Some kind of paint?"

Julia looked closer. "Dried pigments."

"Right. Maybe he's got art ambitions. You know, painting with fish guts." Alex glanced at the jumble of sample blocks. And looked again. "Huh. That's weird."

"What?"

He pulled one out of the pile. "This." He held it next to the paper. "Look at them, the pattern's the same. Like he painted the block to match." Alex turned the block over in his fingers, studying the whitish backside, the altered front. "He really made it look just like sandstone, didn't he? Like the statue." He reached over to open the artifact box and studied the figure inside. "Yeah, he really made it look the same." He brushed his finger over a reddish area on the block that was the shape and size of one on the statue. "Look how close it is." He held the block over the statue, near the red spot. "Same colors, same place. Really close." And then his voice changed. "No way is this an accident."

"Of course not." Julia looked for a moment. "That's probably why he has the statue out—he's using it as a model to mimic the look of sandstone."

"To mimic the look of sandstone or to mimic this statue?" He turned the block slightly, and suddenly the patterns of surface mottling synched up identically. "Not close at all," he murmured. "He's copied it almost exactly."

It took her a moment to process and then she gave him an amused look. "You think he's making a forgery."

"I just think it's weird. I mean look at it. It's not just close, the pattern of mottling is practically identical."

"If Paul Wingate were making a forgery, it *would* be identical."

"Unless he's still getting the hang of it."

"Yeah, well, it's a nice fantasy to pass the time, but you can forget it. Paul's an incredibly well-respected conservator. And very good. Of course he's working with dirt and pigment and mock stone. It's part of his job."

"So what's the statue doing out of inventory without being checked out?" Alex demanded. "What's it doing here at all, if you didn't approve it? What's he doing with isinglass? What's he doing with a wireless card that he hides?"

"Not all that carefully," she reminded him.

"What's he doing hiding it at all? And getting e-mails from your friend the Sphinx, unless he's making merchandise for him to sell."

"Those were spam, Alex," she reminded him.

"Were they? After all, if you're e-mailing someone about forgeries, you're not exactly going to list them by part number."

"Look, Sherlock, there are legitimate explanations for all of this."

Alex crossed his arms. "Sure, you can explain almost anything away if you try. Doesn't it strike you as strange, though? I think we should look around a little more."

"You are *not* going to rifle through his office just on the basis of suspicion," she said hotly. "We have a hard enough time keeping him happy without you giving him another reason to pitch a fit."

"Well, let me add to that suspicion. I just noticed something interesting about the spam."

"What?"

"Look at the preview pane. Did you notice who it's addressed to? Isis53@bluemail.com. It's not his museum address. And take a look at the subject line."

"'Hot and horny teens want to meet you'"

"It's a *reply,* Julia. How many spams have you ever replied to? Now, maybe Paul likes hot and horny teens, but I'm betting not. I think there's something else going on here."

She opened her mouth and then shut it. Her lips tightened. "Spam gets more sophisticated every day, Alex. I'm telling you, conservators are supposed to mimic materials. That's part of their job. You have no idea the mess this could stir up if you insist on carting off and making accusations, especially when it's totally plausible that it's aboveboard."

"Yeah, well, to me it all seems fishy, and not just the isinglass. And maybe you can ignore it but I can't. If there really is something going on here, we need to find out what it is so that we can hit him with it when he comes in tomorrow morning."

Julia gave him an incredulous look. "What do you think this is, some *CSI: Miami*? This is the real world. You don't search people's offices, you don't ransack people's desks, and you sure as hell don't go carting off accusing people of things without being right about it."

"Exactly. Which means I need to find proof."

Julia gave an exasperated sigh. "You need to find a shrink because you're going nuts. Now, I'll be in the book repository. *If* you come across a smoking gun— shoot yourself with it."

"Fine."

"Fine." She stood with her arms crossed, glaring at him. "You can go anytime."

"I will." She didn't move.

"Good." A corner of his mouth twitched. "You've got good eyes if you can read all the way from here."

"I'm warning you…" But she turned on her heel and went.

17

IRRITATION CARRIED JULIA through the first couple hours of work. She knew it would have been easier with Alex's help, but she was damned if she was going to ask him. She'd taken her share of ancient-history courses. She knew how to research, and anyway, she had the electronic index. She'd make out just fine.

Whether she'd find anything, of course, was another question. She was lucky with sources, often finding English translations of earlier works. Where she didn't have translations, the language was usually Latin. Reading it was far from easy, but she was able to stumble along and be reasonably confident she wasn't missing too much.

But she was missing Alex.

She found herself glancing over and over again at his chair. The chair he'd been using, she corrected herself, but she couldn't keep from smiling at the spider he'd made with a few paper clips and an eraser. She missed the companionship, missed being able turn to him and read some particularly interesting tidbit, ask for his opinion on which source to seek next.

He was better at this than she was, she acknowledged reluctantly. And she was better when he was around.

It had been silly to get so ticked off at his wild accu-

sations, no matter how off base they might have been.
She should have just remained amused. Somehow,
though, it had felt like an attack on one of her own. And
it had felt as though Alex were making her a part of it.
Whatever differences she had with Paul, he still
deserved respect, he still deserved the benefit of the
doubt. It was ridiculous to think that he would take such
a risk with his career and his life, particularly right
under her nose.

But deep down inside, she wondered if she were
trying too hard to explain things away. Sighing, she
raised her head from her book just in time to see Alex
step through the door.

And despite herself, felt the quick rush of pleasure.

"Hey," she said.

"Hey, yourself." He walked to his chair, brushing a
hand over her hair as he passed.

And every thought in her head scattered. She took a
deep breath and brought herself back. "So, did you find
your smoking gun?"

He sat, as relaxed as if he were at a baseball game.
"Nope, no smoke to be seen. Everything looks completely normal."

"See?" she said in relief. "I told you—"

"Except for the fact that the bottom drawer on his
desk is still locked."

"Like I told you yesterday, there are any number of
reasons for that."

"That's what I decided, too," he said easily. "So I
thought I'd come in and see if you wanted to kiss and
make up."

She felt a ridiculous smile spreading across her face.
Maybe she'd been angry at his feckless accusations, but
it was hard to stay ticked off for too long. It felt too

damned good to have him there. "You really don't ever give up, do you?" she asked.

"No," he said. "I don't." Abruptly, the smile was gone. Something flickered in his eyes then, something hot and determined, something that dragged her back into memories of the night before, his body hard and naked against hers, his mouth relentless, his back slick under her fingers—

"Get your hands on anything?" Alex asked.

Julia blinked, jerked out of her reverie. "Well. Well," she repeated. "Uh, so far, I know where the White Star isn't. Does that help?"

"It's information."

"I suppose. It's the needle-in-the-haystack thing again. You know how crazy it makes me that we don't have the Internet or at least a comprehensive library?"

He rubbed his knuckles over his jaw, dark now with a weekend's worth of beard. "They wouldn't necessarily help you. Don't forget, not a lot of people really knew about the White Star, except as a legend. Even if we were outside, you'd still have to go to rare-book libraries to track it. Your best bet for now is to do what you're doing, sift through data."

"I've been combing through some histories of Constantinople and stories of the sack, hoping to come across something helpful, maybe a letter or something I could use."

"You ever wonder how the people of the future are going to write the histories of today?" Alex asked idly. "I mean, people don't write letters and keep them like they used to. They don't leave a paper trail."

"There's e-mail," Julia pointed out.

"Sure, but it's here and gone, unless you print it out and most people don't. People don't even keep journals like they did. You won't be able to get a Ph.D. in a hundred years studying the letters of Jonathan Safran Foer because there probably won't be very many of them."

She'd never really thought about it before. "On the other hand, these days most prominent people write their autobiographies."

"Prominent people?" He snorted. "Everyone and their brothers have written their autobiography."

Julia flashed a quick grin. "Signs of the apocalypse."

"Or they write tell-all books. *My Life with Jacko. I was a Famous Person's Chauffeur. Dishing Dirt at the White House.* Wait a minute." He rose abruptly. "That's what we need."

"Dishing Dirt at the White House?" Julia turned to watch him.

"Anecdota Veritas."

"It sounds like a book by some Greek philosopher."

"Nope, it's by a Roman, Sidonius. He was an assistant for Justinian." Alex's teeth gleamed. "Sort of the equivalent of the White House press secretary."

"Justinian, the Roman emperor?"

"Gold star for you." He swooped in to kiss her lightly before continuing his pacing. "He ruled in the mid sixth century, but he wasn't based in Rome. By his time, they'd moved the seat of the empire to—"

"Constantinople," she said simultaneously with him, her lips still vibrating from the touch of his. "How very convenient."

"Isn't it just? Anyway, he mostly stuck to the great-and-noble ruler party line. But after everybody died, the kid gloves came off and he wrote *Anecdota Veritas.*"

"The Kitty Kelly edition?"

"And how." His eyes flashed green with excitement as he warmed to his subject. "This was serious dish, all the scandals about Justinian, his wife Theodora, society, pretty much anything that went down."

"Libelous?"

"If they'd had laws back then. Of course, the fact that all his targets were dead by the time it was published sort of made it moot."

"Timing is everything."

"Absolutely. He made a big deal in his preface about how he couldn't have written it while their evil spies were alive or else he'd have been murdered on the spot."

"And would he?"

"I wouldn't have been surprised. You've got to watch tweaking the tail of a tiger that big." He sent her a sidelong glance. "You can tweak my tail anytime."

Her lips twitched. "I'll keep that in mind. Is the book credible?"

"Yes and no. For years, it was the commonly accepted account. According to him, Theodora made Madame du Pompadour look like an amateur. She had Justinian so completely enthralled he just let his empire fall apart."

"Why would a man throw everything away over a woman?"

Alex looked at her. "When it's the right woman, sometimes a man doesn't have a choice. Sometimes what his head's telling him is the last thing that matters."

For a moment, she couldn't speak, couldn't do anything but look into those green, green eyes.

Then he blinked and released her. "Anyway, the thinking these days is that Justinian and Theodora were decent people and fair rulers. *Anecdota Veritas* is considered mostly exaggeration, if not downright lies."

"So why should we look at it?"

"Because he had a way of throwing in little details

of life in the capital, and maybe, just maybe, he heard something that could help us."

"Let me take a look and see if we have it." She typed the name in and the search results scrolled on-screen.

"He shoots, he scores," Alex crowed. "An English translation, no less."

A corner of her mouth turned up. "Well, go get it, Shaq."

The book's cover was oxblood-red. Alex flipped it open to the table of contents and pulled his chair up next to her. "You gotta love these chapter names. 'How the general was cuckolded by his wife'? 'How the depraved Theodora disported herself'? Maybe we should read that one. You can learn Theodora's double-jointed marmot-juggling trick," he murmured in her ear.

She turned her head a little too quickly and found herself almost lip to lip with him. For a heartbeat, they stared at each other. A fraction of an inch separated them. The merest motion of her head, or his, would have brought them together, would have dragged her into the heat and the madness. His pupils expanded, turning his eyes almost black.

Julia forced herself to take a breath and moved away. "I've forgotten more about marmots than Theodora ever thought of. How about you read something useful, like 'The extravagances of Theodora and her court'?"

But it wasn't there, and it wasn't in "How decadence overtook the wealthy of Constantinople."

"What about 'How Theodora consorted with grave robbers'?" Julia suggested.

Alex flicked her a quick smile, skimming the opening passages, and stopped. "I think we might have something here. 'At this time, one of Theodora's attendants began to boast of a talisman that bestowed sexual potency, which quickly became a topic of great fascination. Charms from Egypt and Persia became the fashion among the ladies, who would wear them openly or string them about the necks of their lovers.

"'A very ambitious trader, Asanius, one day gained audience with Theodora to offer an account of an ancient amulet rumored to exist in Egypt, an amulet able to bestow immense sensual pleasure. It had once belonged to great lovers, he claimed, and had been a treasured possession of the pharaoh Horemhotep. Alas, but upon his death, it had been buried in his tomb with him, for such was the practice with the Egyptians, and his tomb had been lost.'"

Julia stirred. "Horemhotep?" she murmured.

"Yeah. A buddy of Felix's?"

"Late Dynastic period. I don't remember when exactly, but somewhere around 400 or 500 B.C. The Egyptians were barely keeping their heads above water at that point. Lots of invasions by the Persians."

"Are you trying for another gold star?"

Unconsiously, she touched her fingers to her lips, remembering the kiss after the first one. Adrenaline vaulted through her. "Just trying to impress you."

"I'm already impressed," he said softly, leaning toward her.

And she knew that if she kissed him this time, her choices would be gone. "What else does it say?" she asked a little desperately. "The book."

Alex blinked and shook his head a little. "You want to hear more?"

"Yes," she said firmly.

"All right…let's see. 'Theodora decried it as pagan nonsense,'" he read, "'but Asanius spoke persuasively to her of the amulet, until at length she offered him a kingly fortune if he were to produce it for her, demanding always proof that it came from the pharaoh's tomb.'"

"That Theodora, she drove a tough bargain."

"Wait till you read about all the people she had thrown in underground prisons to rot. All that, and she was sexually rapacious, too."

"She must have been quite the multitasker."

"And all without a Day-Timer. So, let's see. 'Some months went by and became a year, and then more passed until it became nearly two, and finally one day, the trader reappeared at the palace. He was burnt dark by the sun and his beard had gone gray, but his clothing was rich and he wore golden cuffs upon his wrists.

"'He told Theodora that he had journeyed to Egypt, where he searched until he found the tomb of the pharaoh Horemhotep. And he delved his way into the tomb, this one deep in the ground, not in a high pyramid, and there did he discover a room full of treasure, and in a golden case, an ivory amulet shaped as a star, with rich carvings. And he produced the case with its signs of Horemhotep, and Theodora pronounced herself well pleased, until she discovered a small flaw upon the back of the amulet, whereupon she refused to pay the trader and had him beaten from the palace.'"

They stared at each other. "Sounds like the crack again," Alex said. "The White Star?"

"Maybe. It's still hard to be sure. The trader could have brought her junk."

He raised a brow at her. "A Moroccan tchotchke?"

"We didn't invent forgeries recently, you know."

"No. We've just been perfecting them."

She gave him a long, level look. "Let's not go there right now."

"All right, I'll give you the end of the story. 'And she, Theodora, this godless wife of our Christian emperor, wore this pagan thing about her neck, this object plundered from a tomb desecrated by grave robbers. But it mattered naught to her. She flaunted it to the pious as she flaunted her body.

"'I would think this amulet an invention of the trader had I not discovered an account in a Greek history of such a charm. It was not reported as a sexual charm, though, but a talisman that brought good fortune to the pure of heart and ill to those opposed. And there was none so impure as Theodora, and accordingly she died not long after, a depraved fiend gone from the world, unloved and unmourned by all who knew her.'" Alex set the book down. "Hey, don't hold back, Sidonius. Tell us how you really feel."

"She was good at making enemies, this Theodora."

"At least one that we know of. Maybe her rapaciousness didn't include the royal press secretary."

From the laboratory came the faint sound of a ringing bell. For a moment, they just looked at one another blankly.

And then they shot to their feet. "The Internet," Julia cried, springing up to sprint toward the door.

18

IN THE OFFICE, ALEX sank down in the chair. "Something's come through on his account." With a click of the mouse, he opened the Web browser. "Okay, let's see if we get lucky. Nypd.gov ought to do it."

Julia stood to one side, looking over his shoulder. "Why don't you use a search engine?"

"I bet this will work."

"Oh, really?" she asked, watching as the URL defaulted to a generic search page. "Hmm, guess you lost that bet. What do I get?"

"A sample of my rapacity?"

"Been there, done that. Why don't you try a search engine?" she persisted as he keyed in another guess. "Oh, wait a minute, I get it. This is one of those guy things, like not asking for directions, right?"

Alex gave a long-suffering sigh. "I don't want to use a search engine because it'll bring up *NYPD Blue* and every other damned thing we don't need."

"Just try it and see. Then you can go back to your guesswork. Search under *NYPD*," she suggested.

Alex keyed in *police* and *new york*.

"What are you doing?"

"See? New York State Troopers, Port Authority of New York, Getting Guns off the Streets…"

"Just do me a favor, search under *NYPD.*"

"Okay." Alex heaved another long-suffering sigh. "There. Are you satisfied?"

"Completely," Julia said smugly and pointed to the first result on the list. "That one, please. The one that says 'Offical New York City Police Department Web Site.'"

Alex glowered at her and clicked. Blue flooded across the screen. "Great. All right, here we are. Gates of heaven. The world at our fingertips. Let's see, you want to see the list of most-wanted felons? Or look up crime statistics? Or maybe buy NYPD gear?"

"I'll settle for 'Contact Us,'" she said, and he clicked on it obediently. The link brought up a page of phone numbers for every precinct in the city. Julia stared. "You've got to be kidding me. They don't have an emergency e-mail address?"

"Maybe they figure if it's really an emergency, you'll call," Alex said mildly.

"What if we don't have a phone?" she snapped.

"Here we go." He clicked on an E-mail Us link.

A page loaded inviting them to write to the police commissioner. "Great," Julia said. "We ought to hear something in what, a week?"

"Okay, who else do we know who can help? You want to go to a Web-mail site and try to get through to family or friends?"

"I don't have anyone's address memorized," she said helplessly. "Do you? I just use their aliases in my address book."

He scrubbed a hand through his hair. "Only work contacts, and they won't be there right now." They stared at each other a moment, nonplussed. "Well, you want to at least buy some NYPD gear?" Alex asked.

"Too late. I think we lost our connection again."

He waved a hand dismissively at it and closed down the browser. "Aw hell, I think at this point it's a sign from God. We're supposed to be in this damned basement. Some way, somehow, we're supposed to learn a lesson. And we won't be released until we do."

"You believe the universe is that focused on you and me?"

"Obviously, you don't."

"I think it's chance. There are too many people on this globe for there to be a path for each and every one."

"Do you believe in fate?"

"Maybe," she said cautiously.

He rested his elbows on the corner of the desk, pushing aside a stack of books and folders. "So by that logic, we got locked in here by chance, but maybe in some way it was kind of fate that it was you and me as opposed to you and someone else, that the universe is throwing us together because it knows that something's supposed to happen with us and we were too close to walking away."

"I'm not sure the theory works that way." Her voice was uneasy.

"You've got to be flexible."

Julia wet her lips. "Alex—"

"It was different last night, Julia," he said softly, rising. "Didn't you feel it? Can't you trust it? Can't you just give it a chance?" He slipped his hands up into her hair, sliding his fingertips through the strands. "Trust me," he whispered, and pressed his lips to hers.

For a long moment Julia stood unmoving, lost in the touch of his mouth. It wasn't a demand, it was a question, an invitation, a spreading warmth that beckoned to her. And she yearned for more, not a desire of the flesh but a desire of the heart.

Alex stepped toward her, slipping his arms around her, and she half turned toward him.

And with a rustle and thump, the pile of books and folders and papers on the corner of the desk fell to the floor.

Julia pulled loose and looked at the mess. "Good Lord, we're tearing apart his office."

"Like he'd notice." Alex moved to pull her into his arms again.

She pushed his hands away and stepped back. "Yes, he would." Kneeling, she began to pick up the pile, stacking up books and handing them over to Alex. "I mean, how would you feel if you walked in and your stuff was all over the floor?"

"That's what he sees every day," Alex said, taking the paperbound conference proceedings she handed him and stacking them neatly. "He'll probably be traumatized to find something straightened up."

Julia reached to scoop up a manila folder that had spun away across the floor, scattering papers around it. "Look at it this way, maybe we'll inspire him to do better." She stacked them, flicking Alex a mischievous glance. "We could convert him, change his life," she continued, turning her attention back to what she was doing.

And froze, staring at the paper in her hand. For a moment she said nothing, only read. Then she began swiftly picking up papers, setting some aside immediately, reading through others rapidly.

"What's up?" Alex demanded. "What are you looking at?"

"Test results," she said slowly. "Materials tests from

the scientific lab." She looked at him. "They're for the statue of Anubis."

"He was analyzing it."

"It looks like it."

He crouched beside her to help her gather the papers. "So what do all these little lines mean? It looks like a picket fence."

"They're EDS data."

"EDS?"

"Part of the scanning electron microscope. It uses light to profile the material in a sample. Those little lines are like the fingerprints of all the materials that make up the statue—silica, iron oxide, whatever. It's an analysis of what a material really is, not just what it looks like. Two materials can look identical but be very different."

"Sort of like steel and tin?"

"Sort of," she agreed. "The EDS can differentiate between them. An EDS plot of steel would have one set of lines, an EDS plot of tin would look very different. The downside is that you have to actually take a tiny physical sample of the piece."

"That's a pretty big downside."

"Oh, it only has to be three or four millimeters, and we usually take it from the bottom, where it won't show. We use the analysis to pick out modern materials, show if a statue is, say, cast stone instead of a Nile Valley sandstone."

"Or help you figure out how to make your cast stone look like Nile Valley sandstone, right? He's using the test results to match his forgery to the real thing."

"Yup." Julia rose and grabbed one of the blocks from the jumble, checking it on all sides. "See the label?" she said excitedly. "These printouts include data for samples labeled A through G. He's testing sample blocks to find a match."

"And then he just molds a new statue and sends it off to his friend."

"Sort of." She paced around the office, searching every available surface. "You know, on one hand, I can't believe he's doing this because I can't imagine someone involved in a criminal act being so careless. At the same time, it makes perfect sense. Who's going to notice? It's all stuff he'd have around anyway. And he's Paul. He marches to his own drummer. No one would suspect him." She paused and stared at Alex. "Including me."

"You came around, though," he said. "I like to think you came around on a lot of things."

But Julia, studying the shelf behind Paul's desk, didn't hear him. Suddenly she spied what she sought, grabbing up a plastic Baggie on a lower shelf. "I'm on to you, Paul," she murmured to herself and turned to Alex. "This is the other part of his art project."

"Dirt?"

"Stone dust. A person selling forgeries isn't going to last too long if they get found out. You can't get an exact spectroscopic match with cast stone because you have to use polyester resin to hold the powdered stone together. Polyester resin, or almost any man-made material, has a radically different spectrum—the set of lines," she elaborated, "than stone and the typical organics used in ancient art. Test an object made with polyester, even a fractional amount, and you'll get a whole bunch of lines in your spectrum that aren't supposed to be there. Plus, polyesters fluoresce differently under UV illumination—they'll look yellow, say, instead of clear. That's where the isinglass comes in."

"What's he doing, coating the statues with stone dust?"

Julia nodded. "And pigmenting them. He can make the coating really thick and able to stand up to mechanical sampling. He could even adhere some excavation dust if he wanted, to make it really authentic. Isinglass is organic, so it isn't going to show up in your data. Presto, he's made an undetectable copy."

Julia threw Alex a furious look. "The son of a bitch is forging our collection."

_19_

ALEX SAT BACK DOWN at the computer. "So maybe we ought to take a closer look at the spam our buddy is getting from his Egyptian correspondent. Maybe there's something buried at the bottom."

Julia drew the second chair over to the desk and sat, heedlessly, on the pile of paper it held. She looked mad enough to spit. "I can't believe he's been doing this. I've been seeing reports of forgeries out there. I would never in a million years have suspected Paul."

Alex clicked on the hot-and-horny-teens e-mail. "So just for kicks, let's see what we've got here." He scrolled to the bottom. "Nothing hidden underneath, it doesn't look like."

"It started with the Sphinx," Julia said. "'Looking for action?'"

"It gets right to the point, you've got to admit. So does Paul's reply. 'Hi, my name's Ani. I'm eighteen with long blond hair and double-D breasts. This is a picture of me with my dog. I play around with him sometimes when I get horny. You should see the things we get up to. I could bring him to see you if you want. You can watch us play and even join in.'"

Julia made a face. "Charming."

"I don't think Paul was suggesting bestiality," Alex said in amusement. "You've got to admit, he gets the tone right."

"So Ani and her dog. Three guesses what picture he sent him."

"It got the Sphinx hot. 'I never knew such hot chicks were around. Your picture is really sexy. I'm showing it to a friend. He really likes dogs.'"

"Maybe this is the way they do business. Paul picks out a likely item and sends it to the Sphinx. He looks around, finds a buyer and they go forward."

"It makes sense. Look at the dates on the e-mails. This all started back in January. Paul answered the Sphinx's message with 'I can't wait,' and it's another month before the Sphinx replies. 'Ani, you are such a babe. My friend really wants to meet you. He is so hung. He'll show you a good time. My number's 105-0706.'"

Julia glanced speculatively at Alex. "The fee?"

"One way a guy could be hung," he murmured, studying the number, trying to remember if any other country besides Canada used a seven-digit phone number.

"This particular piece would probably get something close to half a million dollars at auction. Maybe it's a code. Knock off that last number and you've got a reasonable black market value."

Alex leaned back for a moment and just let himself look at her. Lovely dark eyes, a tumble of dark hair, a mouth that had a way of making him forget his own name. It was no wonder he'd fallen first for her looks, for the slamming sexuality of her that night at the gala in her red dress. Somewhere along the line, though, he'd begun to fall for her mind instead.

And this weekend had just sealed the deal.

Julia was staring at him. "What?"

"Sorry. It's like I told you, smart women are very sexy. And you are one smart woman," he said.

Her cheeks tinted with pleasure. "So, okay, this arrives and Paul swings into production. He gets the statue, tests it and spends some time matching the stone. You know," she said thoughtfully, "all the doors have time locks that track coming and going. We can prove when Paul went into inventory, although again, it's hard to prove it wasn't in the course of his regular business."

"Don't get discouraged," Alex told her. "He's got to have left enough lines dangling to trip himself up. Let's keep going. So he replies, 'I really want to meet your friend. Maybe me and my dog and him can have some fun. My number's 205-0906.' Counter offer?"

"Could be. It's a nice little profit."

"Works for me." Again, the zeros, each number a neat mirror of the others.

"Apparently the Sphinx agreed. 'We can give you all the pleasure you ever dreamed of,'" he says. "'You know where to find me. Just bring yourself hot and horny and ready for action.'"

"And all they have to do is arrange a pickup. Slick," Alex said in reluctant admiration. He took a closer look at Julia. "What's wrong?"

"All of this. I can't believe he's been doing this. How many of our pieces has he forged?"

"It can't be that many. Wouldn't people eventually recognize them from your collection?"

She sighed wearily. "It doesn't work that way. People only know the really important artifacts. We display a fraction of our inventory, and our holdings aren't published anywhere. A lot of them aren't memorable."

"Yeah, but this one's different," Alex argued. There

was something about it, something that drew his eye. He opened the box again and stared at it. "It's special."

"I agree. It caught my eye when we went through inventory last year. The problem is, we acquired a three-foot-tall Anubis statue in 1982, and that's the one we keep out in the Egyptian-sculpture room. There's just too much here to display it all," she said helplessly. "Paul knew exactly what to go after. A piece practically no one but us knows we have."

"That's the problem with inside jobs. You've got someone who knows all the ins and outs."

Julia rose. "Look, Alex, close that up. And the computer. We need to get his office looking like it did when he left on Friday. He can't know we were looking around. He can't know what we've found. Tomorrow morning, as soon as we get out, we go to security and the police."

"No way," he said. "First, we bust open this bottom drawer. Then we put everything back as it was." It was an old desk, oak, from the Thirties or Forties. It would be easy enough to open the lock. Hell, he could probably slip it with a nail file.

"Alex, we're not the right ones to deal with this," Julia said positively. "We shouldn't even be touching anything at this point. I mean, I'm confident you're right, something's going on, but we've only got a suspicion, nothing conclusive."

"That's exactly why we need to see what he's hiding."

"That's exactly why we don't," Julia countered. "The last thing we need to do is compromise more evidence. There's no way any of this would be admissible in court—we've broken in to get it all and we've touched everything. A defense attorney would have a field day. Paul could wind up getting off scot-free. We've got to get someone in here to watch him and catch him at it."

"What, are you going to hide somebody in the closet? Give Felix a camera? Come on. We'll lock it back up after," he wheedled.

"And maybe scratch the lock so he sees we've been in it? No way. What's to stop Paul from saying the forgery's planted? Assuming there's even a forgery in there. That drawer could be empty." She paced restlessly in the small office. "It could have been locked when he inherited the desk and the key was just lost. You know what some of those old desks from the basement are like. Just because it's locked doesn't mean there's anything to find. Maybe he's making these things at home—assuming we're even right about it."

"We *are* right and he's making them here. He's got to be. He has to have the originals as reference," Alex reminded her. "He's got to be doing it here, at least the final part of it, and given the isinglass and the e-mails, he's got to be at the finishing stage with this one."

"Come on, Alex," she pleaded. "Let's shut off his computer and go."

Alex studied her and gave in with a sigh. "All right."

"Cheer up," she said. "We've got another mystery to finish up."

"What's that?"

"The story of the White Star."

HARRY NICKELSON whistled as he walked through the glass door of the employees' entrance to the museum. 'Nother day, another dollar. There were worse jobs than sitting in the guard room all night.

"Afternoon, Dolores," he said to the buxom Latina at the security station. "Always a pleasure."

"What's gotten into you?"

He set his lunch bucket on the counter and waved his

badge before the bar-code reader. "Nice day, the cold weather's goin' away. Can I help it if I'm in a good mood? You know, it's maybe something in the air."

"Yeah, exhaust fumes making you dippy," she muttered, watching the exiting employees stream out.

But he could see her trying not to smile at him. Dolores looked good even when she was rolling her eyes at him. Nice brown eyes, nice mouth, a fanny with a little meat on it. Harry wasn't one of those guys who wanted a woman who looked like a stick. He liked to have a little something to hold on to.

He nudged his lunch bucket aside. "So when are we going to go get a drink?"

She finished checking through the backpack of a coat-check kid who was leaving and gave Harry a look as though he were an unripe melon she was going to hand back at the store. "What, you and me?"

"Who the hell else do you think I mean, we? Of course you and me. Come on, Dolores, I'll show you a good time."

"Ha. Like I need to see your version of a good time. What I need to see is a report in the morning showing what went on during your shift."

"I left a report," he said indignantly.

"Sure, the time you came on shift, the time you went off."

"Yeah, so?" He adjusted his utility belt.

"So what else happened?"

"What, you kidding?" He looked at her as if she were losing her marbles. "Nothing else happened. Nothing ever happens this shift. We just babysit an empty building. Only exciting thing that would happen is maybe you'd say yes to goin' out with me."

A glint of humor flickered in her eyes. "I say yes, it better not show up in your report."

"Then you better expect to time in and time out, only. I'm telling you, nothing happens on this shift, Dolores. Nothing at all."

"I STILL THINK WE ought to be looking at the papyrus scrolls instead of these," Alex said, shifting restlessly in his chair.

Julia glanced over from her copy of Cleisthenes. "Hmm, gee, let's see, do you read hieroglyphs?"

"No. But I think it's time I learned."

"And you really think that out of all the scrolls and all the libraries in the world, some fragment that just happened to mention the White Star would wind up here?"

"I'm just saying…"

"Think about it. We've been told that Adeodatus wrote a poem about the White Star, so we know the legend somehow made it into the classical canon."

"So?"

"So, how did it get there? Someone had to travel and hear the legend, don't you think? I'm thinking our best bet is to look at some of the classical histories and travel accounts of Egypt, see if it pops up."

She knew she was being borderline obsessive, but what else did she have to do with her time? She'd traced it to Constantinople and identified it with the crack. The amulet she'd seen was probably the White Star.

Assuming the trader wasn't a lying shyster, which, of course, there was every possibility he would be.

The reality was, she wouldn't really be able to relax until she'd gone back as far as her sources would let her go.

The time passed and she wished for Alex's cell-phone jukebox, long since out of power. Water or a soda would be good, but there was no way she was bringing any liquid around these books. Even the modern translations still deserved care.

"This is great stuff, you know," Alex said.

"What are you reading?"

"Herodotus. He was looking at some skulls of Persians and Egyptians and wanted to know why the Persian skulls would crumble under a pebble but the Egyptian skulls wouldn't crush. Here's what they told him. 'The Egyptians from early childhood have the head shaved, and so by the action of the sun the skull becomes thick and hard. The Persians, on the other hand, have feeble skulls because they keep themselves shaded from the first, wearing turbans upon their heads.'"

"Who knew that shade was so dangerous?"

Alex eyed her. "I think when we get out of here we should head south, maybe to Aruba, and put you in a bikini to toughen up your bones. I've never seen you in a bikini, you know."

"That's because we got involved in December."

"But we never took a beach holiday," he pointed out. "I think we ought to remedy that. Think of it—sand, blue water, umbrella drinks, sun…. We could toughen up your skull, too, although you don't really need your head to be any harder, now that I think about it," he added, wincing when she punched him in the arm. "Hey, what was that for?"

"I'm not hardheaded," she told him.

"Good, then that means you'll go with me to Aruba?"

His eyes were green and amused on hers. "No," was what she should have told him. But suddenly, for the life of her she couldn't figure out why. "We'll see," was all she said.

Alex bobbed his head as though to a beat only he could hear. "I'll take 'We'll see' for now."

Julia flushed and turned back to her book.

Chapter followed chapter. It took her a moment to realize she'd found it when she finally did, because she was so bleary-eyed from reading, but there it was in front of her. "Alex, I think I found something," she said.

"Read it."

"This is from Cleisthenes."

"Did he have a strong skull?"

She glowered at him. "Do you want to hear this, or not?"

"No, please, read away, my Egyptian beauty."

"All right." She cleared her throat. "'In Cairo, I met a man who taught me much of the land, and I spent many afternoons in congress with him. For though he was now bent and gnarled with age, he had once been a high servant of the pharaoh Horemhotep and had traveled widely in the desert lands beyond. We spoke for long hours as he related to me accounts of empires and feats of arms, of kingly men and strange tusked animals large as a house.

"'And yet it is not, after all, such stirring stories that remain in my thoughts, but a lesser one. The pharaoh Horemhotep was possessed of an amulet of great fascination and power, an amulet once plundered long ago as a spoil of war from a great kingdom now numbered among the vanquished foes of Egypt, and lost among the shifting sands. It was an object of great age, a star of ivory, white and smooth, handsomely carved and all unsullied save for a small fissure on its back.'" She stared up at Alex.

"That's it," she whispered.

"I know. Keep reading."

"'This amulet held great sway over the pharaoh's thoughts, and he sought to know more of it. So he sent his servant into the wide desert, to hunt up the cities of the lost kingdom and find what he may, for surely such a powerful talisman was greatly valued by their rulers. The servant traveled for many days and spoke to the desert nomads who inhabited such places. And he sifted through rumor and legend until finally he reached a half-buried city.

"'And there, among the ruins, he found the words that told the tale of a great love that was not to be and an amulet that held a love so pure it could pass through the ages like a hand through the water of a river.

"'He made to leave, but a great sandstorm arose in the desert, and his camel would not suffer itself to be led but ran away. The searcher struggled mightily and returned to the ruined city, and sheltered there for five days and nights. And on the sixth day, the storm had passed. Of his camel, there was no sign. He walked out into the desert and a band of nomads found him wandering all empty-handed, tormented with thirst, and they conveyed him back to the cities of the living.'"

Julia closed the book, a faint buzzing in her ears. "It's done," she said. "We did it."

20

THEY WERE BOTH SILENT as they walked out of the book repository. They'd tracked the amulet across the millennia, across countries and continents. And now, finally, the story had ended.

"The birth of the legend," Julia murmured as Alex handed her the last can of Coke.

"And as close as we're likely to get to the origin of the White Star." He hopped up on one of the tables and she sat next to him.

"Maybe it's as close as we were meant to get. There are some secrets in the world that should be kept." She took a drink and handed the can to him. "It took a sandstorm to hide them all those centuries ago. Maybe that was a sign."

"More hocus-pocus?"

"It's not hocus-pocus," she flared. "It's real. For good or for evil, the White Star changed people's lives. There are some powers that are that strong." Blinking, she looked down.

"Hey." Alex took a closer look. "Are you okay? What's up?"

She swiped at her eyes in embarrassment. "I'm tired and loopy from all the research. It just gets me, that's all. Imagine loving someone so much that the legend of it travels through the ages, and the token of it still carries all that feeling. And it did. That's not hocus-pocus," she said angrily. "That amulet was more than just inanimate ivory, and you know it. You felt it."

He nodded slowly.

"That's the way love is supposed to be. It's not supposed to be about going hunting for a Dutch model when you have a midlife crisis or about control. It's supposed to be about the feeling that lives in that amulet."

Alex set down the can of soda. Maybe the Dutch model was part of the reason she guarded her emotions so jealously, part of the reason she relied so much on her intellect—she'd seen, after all, where living by the heart alone could lead a person. "So how did your father explain the Dutch model to you?" he asked softly.

There was no real surprise there, which told him a lot. "Gerald? He didn't bother. But then, he was never very present in our lives. I haven't heard from him since I got my Ph.D. He sent me a card with a hundred-dollar check," she elaborated, and picked up the can of soda to take another drink.

"Nice."

"He actually showed up when I got my B.A., Helga in tow."

"Helga?"

"Helga, Heika, Sonia Henie," she said carelessly. "It's hard to remember."

Alex studied her. "You're still ticked at him."

"Me? Ticked?" Her laugh was genuine. "I was a child of the eighties—I got therapized within an inch of my life to be sure I coped with it. Which didn't, of course, stop me from marching right out and marrying a father figure, with predictable results."

"Tell me about him."

"Who? Gerald?"

"Your husband."

"Ex-husband," she corrected.

"Ex-husband."

"I'll take state capitals for a hundred, please, Alex."

"Nope. I'm not letting you off the hook on this one. What happened?"

She sighed. "I was young, he wasn't. End of story. Want to split that last protein bar?"

Alex handed it to her. "Come on, keep going."

Julia ripped open the package with a scowl. "I met him when I was finishing my undergraduate degree. He was a visiting scholar. He was so smart. He knew about…everything, it seemed. He'd have these dinner parties with all kinds of intellectuals and they'd talk about real things. They weren't like the people I'd known."

"Like?"

"Like the society people." She handed him his half of the bar. "I mean, if I never go to another one of Bunnie Bernaldo's parties, it'll be too soon. All the same brainless people having all the same conversations," she said impatiently, "wearing five- or ten-thousand-dollar evening gowns they'll put on exactly once and never again so that they can be one up on the rest of the fashionable crowd.

"Edward's world wasn't like that. It was meeting famous artists and authors and playwrights, talking around the table for hours. I felt like I was alive for the first time. And I felt special that he opened the door and let me in, that he thought I was worthy. I couldn't believe it when he proposed." She set the bar aside.

"How old were you?" Alex asked quietly.

"Twenty-two. It was my senior year in college. I was

just…stunned. And a lot of it was hero worship, I know that now. He made me want to be more than I was, better. And I thought that I was in love because isn't that what love is? Caring more for someone else than you do yourself, wanting to be the best possible version of yourself for them?"

Alex nodded. "'Trying to always live up to the best within you,' I believe you said."

She let out a breath. "And so long as I was starry-eyed, everything was perfect. I was the adoring pupil at his knee, absorbing every bit of knowledge he dispensed, being his audience. And he taught me a tremendous amount. But I was learning things elsewhere, too.

"I was midway through my doctorate the first time I corrected him on something. We were having a dinner party and he'd said something about Egyptian art from the Early Dynastic period. But he was wrong. I'd just done some research on it. So I just spoke up and made my point, backing it up with data, the way he'd taught me."

Alex could imagine her, so caught up in the thrill of knowing, of learning, of sharing.

"I was so proud of myself," she continued. "And I thought he'd be proud of me. He didn't say anything, though, just got really quiet. Dinner ended early. And after everyone went home, we had our first fight. About loading the dishwasher, of all things. Except it wasn't about loading the dishwasher at all. It took me years to realize that."

"He wanted an audience," Alex said, wanting badly to hit something. "You weren't supposed to outgrow him."

"I thought he wanted a wife," she said, old pain echoing in her voice. "I thought he wanted an equal."

"Maybe he thought he did."

She moved her shoulders. "Mostly he just wanted to control me, especially toward the end. The more I turned into my own person, the more he wanted to call the shots. I left for my postdoc in Cairo, and it was such a relief to be out from under his thumb. And that was the beginning of the end."

"How long were you gone?"

"A year. I missed him, though. I took an early flight home and went over to the university to surprise him." Her mouth twisted. "I still remember walking up to his open door and hearing his laughter. It reminded me of the good times. And I thought, we'd had them once, and maybe again…. But then I came around the corner and there he was, sitting on the edge of his desk and smiling at some little undergraduate."

He wanted to crush the idiot she'd been married to for putting that look in her eyes. He wanted to pace, to burn off at least some of the anger for her. But he was afraid that if he moved, she'd stop talking, and he didn't want to take that chance. "He didn't deserve you," he said instead.

"Nothing had happened, he told me later, in the middle of the biggest, ugliest fight we'd ever had." She laughed humorlessly. "The hell of it was, I believed him—physically. Emotionally, she was giving him what he wanted, the same thing I had, once. Pure adoration. The sad thing was that I admired him as much intellectually as I had when we'd first met. I didn't admire him as a person, though—the fights, the nastiness, the control games had burned it all out of me. We staggered on for another year, mostly because I was too stubborn to give up. But when I was done, oh boy, I was done."

Alex let out a breath he hadn't been aware he was holding. "What did your aunt Stella think of him?"

"She only met him once. By the time we started dating, she was already ill. Heart disease," she said in answer to his unspoken question. "I could tell by the way she reacted that she didn't think much of him. He went with me to her funeral. It was the first time he met my family. In a way, that was when I really started falling for him."

"Trading one mentor for another?"

She gave him a startled look. "If you like. I missed her so much, and here was Edward, being strong, showing me there was a life outside of the one my family lived. Bad timing. My mother tried to control a lot of what I did and then Edward did. When I broke up with him, I went a little nuts for a while. That was when you and I got together."

And when she was done with her period of madness, she wanted to be done with him. But he wasn't going to let it happen.

Alex stirred. "Can I ask you something? The first night we got together, at the museum fund-raiser, you wore a red dress. This really deep, really wild red. I'd never seen you wear anything like it before."

Julia smiled. "That was my Declaration-of-Independence dress. The divorce had been final for about two months. I'd gotten past the living-hell part, but I was still making my decisions like I had to worry about keeping Edward happy. And then I was in a changing room and the clerk brought in the dress. It was the sort of thing I'd never pick out, but I was in a hurry and I was desperate, so I put it on. And it looked…"

"Amazing," Alex supplied. "It about stopped my heart when I saw you."

Her eyes lit up. "My first thought was that it was way too outrageous, way too tight and low-cut. And all of a sudden I realized that that was Edward talking. And I just snapped. I thought, you know, I'm going to start living for me. I'm not going to live for Edward and I'm not going to follow my mother's life, I'm going to do what I want. And somewhere, I could hear Stella cheering."

"It showed, you know," he said, voice husky with the memory. "The minute you walked through the door that night, you were practically vibrating with it."

"Vibrating with what, 'Take me to bed'?"

"No. Vibrating with…I don't know, confidence. You were putting yourself out there, all of you. Before that, you'd always seemed very reserved and severe. I mean, I noticed you were gorgeous." He reached out to stroke her cheek. "It's kind of hard not to. But I'd never have made a move on you. You were too…"

"Boring?" she supplied bleakly.

He dismissed it with a snort. "No. Focused, maybe. Like there would be a pop quiz at the end of the evening. Like I hadn't done enough to earn the time of day from you. And when you showed up at the gala that night, that was all gone. I looked at you and you were just there, in the moment."

"It was the first time you'd ever approached me outside of work."

"I couldn't have stayed away if I'd tried." He caught her hand.

And she didn't pull away but slipped closer to him. "We were a good pair that way. Both reckless. You were the perfect playmate, the person I could do anything I'd dreamed of with."

"So what happened?"

She sighed and looked at the ceiling. "It was a phase, Alex. I realized that when I was jumping out of the plane last weekend."

"Fine time to have an epiphany."

"Hey, can I pick 'em? Anyway, I figured enough with being crazy, living without thinking. I figured it was time to get my life together. And I thought that meant you, too."

"And what do you think now?" he asked, searching her face.

"I don't know." She let out a long breath. "I know things are different, you're right about that. And I don't know if walking away is the right thing anymore."

He was almost afraid to move, afraid to breathe, afraid any reaction would disturb her, frighten her back from the place she now was.

"I think things through, Alex," she said gently. "That's the way I've always been. Except for the last six months. That's all been about doing what felt good at the time."

"Does it have to be one or the other? Can't you do both?"

"I don't know. It scares me. Maybe that's why I think through a decision and then stick with it. Then again, I stuck with Edward for a long time after I should have, just because I thought I should."

Reaching out, Alex put his hands on her shoulders and turned her gently toward him. "Give it a chance, Julia, that's all I'm asking," he said, fighting to keep his voice casual. "I think we've had something special here this weekend. Let's just take it for a test spin in the outside world and see where it takes us."

She didn't have to say anything; he saw the words he'd hoped for in her eyes. And when he slid off the table, she followed him and flowed into his arms.

In six months, they'd had sex in every conceivable position and place, flouting more than a few laws and rules of propriety. They'd had sex inside and they'd had sex outside, in beds, in cars, against walls, on balconies. In public and in private.

But they'd never made love. When he took her in his arms now, it was with a tenderness he'd never found in himself before. Gentle touch led to gentle touch. He used all the ways he'd learned her body in order to pleasure her. And in a sort of dreamy bliss, she went with it, and pleasured him, too.

For the first time that weekend, they came together naked. For the first time ever, they came together with no barrier between them, with complete trust. And when he laid her down on the pallet and slid into her, it was the next best thing to prayer that he'd ever experienced.

And when he slipped over the edge, he knew he'd slipped into love.

AND SHE DREAMED of the desert, the wind in her hair, the hot night air….

And love.

It flowed through her like a gift. Her heart exploded with the feeling, as though there weren't enough room for it in her breast. In her hands she held the White Star and she watched the golden light flow from her and into it until it began to pulse and glow and vibrate. All there was of her, all there was of her beloved, of the two of them together, locked into the amulet.

Her and Alex.

A feeling that would last for always and forever.

21

ALEX LAY AWAKE, staring into the darkness. Sleep, which hadn't been exactly easy the whole weekend, remained elusive. He could hear Julia's even breathing, feel the warmth of her body against his. She had managed to drift off; for him, it was proving impossible.

He forgot about trying and instead concentrated on the softness of her in his arms, the silky feel of her hair. They'd dressed again after making love; when they woke, it would be Monday, after all, and the conservators would be coming in to free them.

Including Paul Wingate.

It was too soon. As sick as he was of being cooped up, Alex didn't want it to end. This was their time, his and Julia's. He couldn't help feeling uneasy at the prospect of the outside world invading it. He couldn't entirely suppress a superstitious fear that everything would change.

It wouldn't, he reminded himself. This had been a long time coming and it was solidly here. Twenty-four hours, he promised himself, in twenty-four hours, they'd be in this same position, in his bed or hers, and he'd be holding her against him, naked and silky-smooth, and drifting off to sleep to wake together and do it again.

But for now, sleep stubbornly refused to come.

Lying on concrete could have been a factor, of course. Being stiff in over ninety percent of his body could have been another. He shifted slightly. The way he was lying was somehow uncomfortable. Julia was cradled against him, head pillowed on his chest. And the more he tried to lie still and not disturb her, the more his body clamored to move.

Holding his breath, he shifted again, this time actually finding a position that worked. Julia muttered and rolled over to drape one arm across him. That would do it. Now he'd be able to drift off. He closed his eyes.

Seconds ticked into minutes, minutes marched toward the hour. And slowly, insistently, discomfort built again.

Finally, he gave up, disentangling himself slowly from Julia and rolling away. Sleep just wasn't going to happen. There was no point in trying to force it. There was no point in waking her. He rose.

Alex just stood, letting his eyes adjust to the darkness as he decided where to go. The book repository? He'd satisfied his appetite for ancient sources for the moment. Then again, there was no sense in trying to fool himself. He knew where he wanted to go. He knew what he really wanted to do.

He wanted to look in Paul Wingate's office.

No wonder he hadn't been able to sleep.

They'd turned off the computer and put everything back in order. The drawer was off-limits—he'd promised Julia he wouldn't touch it, even though his fingers itched to get at the lock. All he was going to do was sit in there for a while and read maybe. And if he looked around a little while he was in there, just to see if anything jumped out at him, that wasn't a crime, was it?

He doubted Julia would see it that way.

The light seeping in from the corridor was faint, but Alex could see well enough to creep toward Paul's office. Reality was, it would drive Julia nuts if she knew he was looking around again, even if he didn't touch a thing. But it was going to drive him nuts if he didn't.

He felt the void of the doorway ahead of him and stepped cautiously, moving his feet only an inch or two at a time, careful not to brush against anything. Finally, he was inside. Breathing a silent sigh of relief, he closed the door and reached for the switch, squinting in the sudden wash of light.

The office was no less chaotic, but somehow he felt almost at home when he sat down in Paul's chair. After all, he'd spent enough time there in the past few days. Leaning back, he tried to look at the room through Paul's eyes. Jumbles of books, stacks of paper, tools. Baggies of excavation dirt. The laptop.

Alex reached out thoughtfully and fingered the airline ticket that leaned between the sample blocks and the box of gloves. Reims again? he wondered. He'd forgotten to ask Julia where the conference was this year. The prospect that she would be gone within a day or two gave him an unexpected twinge. She'd be back within a week, he reminded himself. Only a lovesick putz would think about following her.

Then again, it had been a while since he'd been to Europe.

Thoughtfully, he picked up the envelope and pulled out the itinerary and receipt. Not Reims, this time. Heidelberg. Departing 5-08-06, arriving 5-09-06, at least Wingate was. And Julia was leaving the next day. Maybe there was a way to arrange some time after, though.

050906. Alex frowned. Where had he seen that combination of numbers? 050906. Each number, spaced by zeros, the nine mirroring the six, the five mirroring... What? He studied the pattern of numbers. 050906. And blinked.

The spam. Not payment negotiations.

Delivery dates.

Paul was leaving that evening to bring the forgery to the Sphinx.

His first thought was to tell Julia, but she was asleep outside in the lab. Anyway, he knew what she would say. Be patient. Wait, talk with security, do it through official channels.

And she'd be absolutely right.

He pulled a scalpel out of Paul's coffee mug of tools and took a closer look at the drawer. He hadn't been kidding with Julia when he'd said he'd specialized in lock picking. As a kid fascinated with detective mysteries, he'd made it his business one summer to learn how locks worked—as many different kinds as he could— and then, of course, to pick them. The lock on the drawer wouldn't take much.

But he'd promised Julia.

Alex drummed his fingers on the desk. *To live up to the best within you.* He laid down the scalpel with a sigh. He'd made an agreement and he'd keep to it. He owed her that. He owed it to himself.

Instead, to distract himself, he opened the storage box that held the statue, unable to resist taking one more look. He could see why Wingate had chosen it. And why it had been snapped up so quickly. It was a compelling figure, foreign, mysterious. To look at it was to feel a breath of the past.

No wonder he'd forged it.

On impulse, Alex pulled out a pair of gloves and put them on. Then he pulled the statue from its padding.

The stone was surprisingly heavy, solid and smooth. Alluring to touch. There was something vaguely disquieting about the eyes. The artist had done exceptional work, bringing the jackals' face to life, investing it with a cool, assessing gaze that must have sent a shiver down the spine of the true believers back when.

Someone had sat in his workshop, smoothing the heavy stone with file and rasp, working at it until it pleased the eye, pleased the hand. It had sat in someone's home or in a temple. The staring eyes, the narrow muzzle were a reminder of what waited.

And now it was here in his hands. And would be here in the museum, hopefully, long after he was dust.

Horsewhipped. Paul Wingate should have been horsewhipped for damaging a work like this in order to execute his crime, no matter how small the chip. No matter how small the chip, the statue was changed forever, he thought, turning it idly over in his hands. No matter how small the chip, it was missing something.

And then he froze.

It wasn't missing something, he realized. It wasn't missing anything. The surfaces were perfectly smooth, even the bottom. Wingate hadn't taken the sample from this figure. He hadn't done any testing on it.

Alex was holding the forgery.

Which meant that Wingate was taking the original.

Adrenaline flooded through him. This was big. Huge. If forgeries could damage the museum's reputation, how much worse was it to lose artifacts from the collection? How much more damaging to know that objects from the inventory—items on display even—could now be fakes?

Rising, he strode to the door. He had to tell Julia, middle of the night or no. He grabbed the doorknob—

And heard the faint clank of a key in the corridor outside the lab.

His heart vaulted in his chest. It wasn't security. There had been no knock, no words, no jingling of their kit. And at nearly four in the morning, it wasn't just any conservator coming in to work early.

Swiftly, Alex spun back to the desk and grabbed the scalpel. Slipping the latch on the locked drawer took only a single flick of the wrist. A quick search revealed what he sought, the bundle of cloth with the same surprising heaviness as the statue—forgery—that now sat on the desk. And a quick glimpse inside the cloth revealed the statue of Anubis.

Quickly he whirled to escape just as he heard the sound of the main door opening. Just as the lights flickered on.

JULIA SAT BOLT UPRIGHT on the pallet, heart hammering, blinking in the flood of the fluorescent bulbs.

"What the…*Julia?* What the hell are you doing here?" Paul Wingate stared down at her, black-bearded, with the face of some medieval ascetic and the stripped-down build of an obsessive distance runner. From her position he appeared far taller than his five foot nine.

Alex was gone. The realization flashed through her as she rose groggily to her feet. "We got locked in," she said, squinting as her eyes adjusted.

"We?" Shock still reverberated in Paul's voice.

"Alex Spencer from Marketing." Alex, who'd disappeared. Operating on instinct, she didn't look around for him. "What time is it?" she asked, instead.

"About four."

"Four?" She blinked. "What are you doing here at this hour?" *And what were you hoping to accomplish unnoticed?*

He shrugged. "I leave for Heidelberg this afternoon. I thought I'd come in early, get some work done. Have you been in here all weekend?" he asked, still incredulous, still trying to get his head around it.

She nodded. "I was down here Friday evening to research an amulet a woman brought in for identification. Someone took the amulet while I was…distracted, and locked us in. The phones are dead, so whoever it was must have done something to them, too." And she saw the tumblers clicking as Paul's mind processed the possibilities.

He frowned at her. "This all sounds pretty bizarre, Julia."

"Oh trust me, I know. But it happened."

"That's too bad," he said absently, but his eyes were already turned toward the back of the lab and his office.

"We had to kind of ransack the place for food. I hope you don't mind, but we used your coffee."

"What do you mean, you used my coffee? My office was locked."

"We broke in," she said, watching him closely.

He spun to her, his brows drawn together. "You broke into my office?" For an instant, the mask slipped to show anger.

And alarm.

"Paul, we were in here for two and a half days. We had to do something."

"The hell you did," he said brusquely, already moving single-mindedly toward the back of the lab. "That office was locked for a reason."

"Really?" Julia asked, studying him. "What was that?"

But he didn't answer, just walked swiftly around the corner to see his office door open, the light on. Shock stopped him for a moment as he stood at the threshold, eyes riveted on the desk. "What have you—"

"Looking for this?" Alex stepped out of the bathroom beyond, holding the figure of Anubis, partially swathed in its cloth.

Paul's head snapped around, every line of his body shouting alarm. "What are you doing holding that, you idiot? That belongs in a storage box."

"Yep, it sure does," Alex agreed.

He was wearing gloves, Julia saw in bewilderment. Looking past Paul's shoulder into his office, she saw the storage box lying open, the figure of Anubis inside it. And felt a surge of anger.

"It's been real interesting, being stuck in this lab for a few days," Alex was saying. "We wound up with a lot of time on our hands. Gave us a chance to take a poke around a little. Amazing what you can find."

"This is outrageous," Paul blustered. Julia moved up alongside him, close enough to see the quick shift of his eyes. "You're lucky I don't call security in right now."

"Go ahead," Alex invited. "In fact, we'll go upstairs with you. I think they'll be interested to hear what we've found. You don't seem to be, though," he observed. "Why is that? Why don't you want to know why we've got two of the same statue here?"

Paul tensed. "You obviously brought one in."

"I think you know that's not true. And the museum curator's here to testify to it."

"You've been a part of ransacking my office, Julia?" he demanded, turning to her.

But Paul's eyes were on the door to the corridor.

"You've had a good little system going here, Wingate." Alex stepped forward. "How many pieces have you cleared out of the museum's inventory?"

"I don't know what you're talking about," Paul snapped. "Give that to me."

"Not a chance," Alex said. "Besides, what are you worried about? You've got another one right there."

Paul's eyes flicked toward Alex and then the door. Before Julia could react, he'd grabbed the vertical support of the open lab shelf next to him and given it a hard shove to send it tumbling down in front of Alex. Bottles of chemicals burst; artifacts skidded across the floor.

And Paul spun for the door.

Julia lunged for him as he went by but he shook her off. Behind her, Alex clambered over the shelf but her focus was on Paul. They had to catch him before he escaped. She ran after him, hot on his heels, around the corner, toward the door.

Close, he was almost there.

Paul's arm flashed to the side and he grabbed at the wheeled table with Felix. He yanked it. And rolled the bulky table right into her path.

Julia cried out. Skidding, she careened into the table, shoving it around in a half circle. The impact sent her sprawling over it and jolted Felix partway off.

"Catch him!" Julia cried as Alex raced up behind her. He moved to get around to the door.

"Not Paul, *Felix,*" she cried, groping desperately for the fragile mummy as he dangled half off the table.

And they heard the snick of the bolt shooting home.

"WHAT THE *HELL* did you think you were doing?" Julia had never been so furious in her life. She didn't know she could get so angry.

She stared at Alex. "I don't even know where to start. I'm so mad right now, I can't think straight."

Felix was back in place, though much the worse for wear. And the door was absolutely, indubitably locked.

"Calm down, Julia. We've got the statue."

"We've got the statue?" Her voice rose. "We've done irreparable harm to an Eighteenth Dynasty mummy, damaged I don't know how many artifacts, gotten locked in again. And all you can say is that we've got the statue? You promised me, you *promised* me that you wouldn't break in there," she said furiously. "But no, you had to do it. You had to be the one. Alex the golden boy cracks the case, only he loses the crook while he's at it."

"I didn't plan for Paul to get away." Irritation flared in Alex's voice.

"Were you *there* for the conversations we had yesterday?" she raged. "Let's get the authorities in here, I said and you agreed. You *agreed*. And then the minute I fall asleep, you're in here breaking into the desk." Unable to stand still, she paced away.

"Look, I didn't intend to break into the desk. I just went in there to look around."

"And the drawer fell open by itself. Well, how about that?" Her voice was scathing. "You know, I must have been out of my mind to buy into your act. I know what you're like, Alex, I *know* it. And I let myself fantasize that somehow everything was different. Well, it's not. You go carting off and do things without any regard for the consequences. It's all about you and what you want. You don't use your head. You never have."

"Did it ever occur to you to ask why I broke into the desk?" He stepped forward, looking as angry as she. "He wasn't just forging, Julia. He was making the forgeries to sub into our inventory and selling off the originals."

Shock stopped her for a moment and then fury bubbled up again. "And you couldn't be bothered to tell me?"

"When did I have time? Paul came in right when I figured it out. He was taking the statue to Heidelberg to deliver it to the Sphinx, that's what the phone numbers meant. Not prices, delivery dates. I had to do something," he snapped. "If I hadn't, I'll tell you what would have happened—you and I would have gone to security, and by the time we managed to convince someone to listen to us, Paul would have been long gone. And the museum would have lost an Old Kingdom statue. I did what I thought I had to do."

"And I hope you're happy with the way it worked out," she said bitterly, looking at the door.

22

ALLARD SQUINTED into the morning sun, wishing for his sunglasses, wishing for the cloak of darkness. Darkness was his home. Darkness was his safety. But then, his foes knew that. They had given him no chance of escape, but kept him bound and under guard throughout the long day and the longer night.

He dismissed the pain in his aching shoulders. It did not matter. What mattered was finding the opportunity. What mattered was gaining control of the situation.

And then they would be sorry.

The vehicle stopped at the bank. With the muzzle of a gun pressed to his ribs, he slid out the door to the pavement, where the tall one was waiting. To passersby, he knew, nothing appeared amiss as he approached the front door of the bank, flanked by his escort.

They thought they had control. It did not matter. He would bide his time and he would seize his moment, and slip through their fingers.

First Bank of Manhattan, the letters were engraved deep into the marble facade of the building. Mighty pillars flanked the entrance, giving the illusion of strength, security. And inside, the White Star.

If they thought he was giving her over to them, they were mad.

In the lobby, he stopped. "Very well. I will go into the vault and retrieve the package. You will wait for me here."

The muzzle of the gun dug into his ribs. "We will go with you."

Allard smiled faintly. "As you wish."

The blonde was at the service desk, and he smiled as he approached her. "So we meet again, Caroline." He pulled out his wallet with its access card.

She beamed. "Why hello, Mr. Allen."

"Good morning. I wish to enter my safe-deposit box." He showed her his card and his identification. "My friends will come with me."

She bit her lip. "Oh, I'm sorry, we can't do that," she said. As he'd expected. "If they're not on the contract, they'll have to wait here."

He clicked his tongue and resisted the urge to gloat. "Alas, my friends, you must wait." It was the opportunity he'd been counting on. They would wait and he would slip out the back door. It was one of his specialties. A chance to elude them, a chance to survive.

A chance to escape with the White Star.

"There is no exception?" the stocky one demanded, an edge in his voice.

"Well…" The clerk glanced over at the tellers.

"Do not worry, *chérie,* we don't mind," Allard said to her kindly.

It was his undoing.

"I suppose we can find one way around it," she told him, eager to please. "We can amend the contract to list them, as well, then change it back. If you want to."

"That would be most kind of you," the stocky one

said before Allard could reply. "Let me give you my identification."

And Allard's pulse began to thud in his ears.

FOR THE THOUSANDTH TIME, Alex checked his watch. He sat in a lab chair by the door, staring at the heavy oak door, with its glossy black knob. Waiting in silence.

Waiting for release.

The air still smelled faintly of acetone and alcohol, even though Julia had started up the fume hoods to suck up the worst of the vapors. After the meltdown, they'd worked for a couple of hours to clean up the spills and put the shelf back in order. It was amazing, Alex reflected, how much two people could accomplish without a word, when they were sufficiently motivated.

One of the tables held a little pile of the artifacts that had been scattered when Paul had overturned the shelf. Most had survived.

Too bad the same couldn't be said for whatever had been between them.

How the hell had everything gone south so completely? Alex wondered in disgust as he and Julia waited side by side like strangers. One moment, all had been well in his life. The next, everything had gone to hell in a handbasket.

But it really hadn't been well. That had been an illusion. He'd thought that Julia had finally decided to believe in him, that she'd finally looked at him and really seen. She accused him of posing, but the pose was hers. When things had gotten toughest, the facade of an open mind that she'd put on had been ripped away and she'd gone back to her easy assumptions.

How did you build a relationship with someone who didn't believe in you? he wondered wearily. The answer was, you didn't. It was impossible. Reality was, they'd never really had a chance to begin with. The knowledge should have made him feel better.

Instead, he felt like hell.

The sound of footsteps in the hallway broke into his thoughts. Instinct had both of them shifting to stare at one another; the events of the past four hours had them turning back to the door.

The brisk slap of shoes on marble came to a stop before the lab door. "What the…?" someone muttered. Alex listened tensely as the key outside rattled in what had become a tiresome ritual. Then, the door opened and a pretty woman with short brown hair stood blinking at them.

"Julia? Alex? What are you doing here?"

THE OVERHEAD LIGHT GLARED off the white walls and white floor of the vault, off the metal banks of safe-deposit boxes with their keyholes like staring eyes. And Allard stood, key in hand. It was impossible that this was what it had come to.

Impossible, now, that he had to relinquish the White Star.

Renouf's men stood vigilant. There was no chance of escape, he thought, here where a bullet would ricochet endlessly off the case-hardened steel. This was not the place to try. Instead, he turned his key and heard the metallic click that released his box.

The cramped little privacy room held only a table and two chairs. With the door closed, it was nearly suffocating. Allard remembered standing at a pet-shop window as a boy, watching a mouse that had been dropped into a cobra's clear glass enclosure for feeding. As soon as its feet had hit the sand and stone, the mouse had tensed, not recognizing the scent perhaps, but knowing instinctually that something was very wrong. And Jean had stared as the mouse scurried around the end of the cage, realizing its peril.

Realizing there was no way out.

Trembling with fear, the mouse had darted from corner to corner, increasingly frantic as the cobra coiled and slid its hooded head ever closer.

Moving in for the kill.

Absurde. Such thoughts would not help. He was not *La Souris Noire,* the dark mouse, but the cobra, biding its time, in control.

Keeping that thought in mind, he set the box on the table and sat. The stocky one settled in a chair; the tall one leaned against the door, watching impassively.

Allard laid his hands on the top panel of the box. It was necessary, he reminded himself. Preservation at all costs. If he must give her up to survive, then he must give her up. There were, after all, other prizes.

His goal now was to walk away alive.

He swallowed and opened the panel, expecting to see the brown wood grain of the museum container.

And the blood drained from his face.

The blank steel of the box gleamed, smooth and featureless under the overhead lights. It was formed without a seam, with no cracks, he could see. He could see because there was no wooden cube inside to interrupt his view. There was no museum container.

The box was empty.

The White Star was gone.

JULIA SAT IN THE INTERVIEW ROOM at the police precinct, unbearably weary. She and Alex had gone straight from the conservation lab to security, telling the story first to underling after underling as they'd waited for the department head to arrive.

Yes, the amulet she'd signed for was gone. No, they had no idea who might have taken it. Yes, it was very old and valuable. Yes, there was every indication Paul Wingate had forged one or more pieces from the museum inventory. Yes, it was possible he had stolen items. No, she had no idea how many pieces might be involved. Yes, she realized they should not have tampered with evidence.

This last, with a glare at Alex.

They'd gone round and round until the department head had come in at nine. At that point, they'd begun it all over again. Julia knew they'd turned a corner when the head had agreed to follow them down to the lab and see the evidence himself.

And now, finally, she sat in the interview room at the local police precinct. She'd let Alex go first; it was her turn now.

Alex… Equal parts fury and loss sloshed about within her, and over it all, a thick layer of self-recrimination. How much of a fool could she be? How could she have believed in him, fallen for the act? And how, when she'd tried to be so smart, could she have gotten in so deep in just three days?

A week before, she'd come back from skydiving resolved to clean up her life. Instead, she'd made more of a mess of it than ever.

So why did she still miss him so much?

The door opened, jarring her from her thoughts. A tall detective in a moss-colored button-down and khakis came in. "Ms. Covington? Sam Mason," he said, holding out his hand.

Julia shook it, frowning at him. With his sandy-brown hair and gray eyes, he seemed familiar, but for the life of her she couldn't say why.

He gave her a quizzical look. "Is there a problem?"

"Have we ever met?" she asked.

"I don't think so, no." His voice was matter-of-fact, his gaze flat and impassive. "I'm one of the officers investigating the Stanhope Auction House robbery. I understand you have some information that might help. You want to tell me about it?"

"A woman brought an amulet into the museum last Friday. A Marissa Suarez."

"Do you have her contact information?"

Julia blinked. "In my office. I can get it for you tomorrow. She wanted to see if I could identify the amulet. She had a suspicion that it might be the White Star, one of the items—"

"I'm familiar with the White Star," he interrupted. "Did Ms. Suarez say how she obtained the object?"

"I think she'd better tell you that part of the story," Julia returned calmly. "I can tell you that I determined conclusively that the amulet she brought me was indeed the White Star."

He studied her. "Do you get that kind of thing often in your line of work, people off the street coming in to ask you to identify objects?"

Julia almost smiled. "More often than you would think, though usually with less interesting results. In this case, though, she was referred. By the sister of one of my colleagues," she elaborated. "Alex Spencer."

"The guy who's here with you."

"He's not with me," Julia corrected tersely.

Mason watched her a moment with those gray eyes.

"My mistake. So why don't you tell me about what happened this weekend?"

There wasn't, Julia thought, enough time in the world...

ALEX SHIFTED on the hard chair in the waiting area at the precinct. He'd finished giving his statement. "You're free to go," they'd told him. If he'd left then, he'd be at home by now, crashed out on his bed, dead to the world.

Instead, he was sitting here staring at scarred walls the color of a manila folder and trying to find a comfortable position on the world's hardest chair. Instead, he was here waiting for Julia out of some perverse chivalric code that said they were in this together and she shouldn't have to walk out alone.

A sentiment she likely wouldn't thank him for.

"You putz, Spencer," he muttered to himself. How was it that after all that happened, he was still hung up on her? Didn't a smart guy get it after a while? Didn't a smart guy give up? But he couldn't quite make himself do it. He couldn't quite give up that last little hope.

He'd wait for her and see what happened. If they were still in détente, then that was it. Enough. She'd go off to Heidelberg and he'd go off to Club Pickup and find himself a woman who appreciated him for a change.

And consign Julia Covington to his past, where she belonged.

"SO DO YOU HAVE ANY IDEA why Wingate might have started up this whole scheme?" Detective Mason asked.

Julia sipped some of the water he'd gotten for her and sighed. "Conservation is kind of a strange profession. It seems really glamorous and exciting when you see it on an A&E doc—" She hesitated. He didn't exactly look like the A&E type. "When you see it on television," she amended. "But in reality, it's hard, low-profile work. If you're a conservator, you're in service to the collection. If you do a perfect job, your contribution is invisible."

"And you think he's looking for something more."

"Paul's a complex guy. He's got a huge ego, for one thing. Status really matters to him. I kind of get the impression he got into this career expecting a really different life than it turned out to be, and he's angry. He lobbied to be appointed a director a couple of years ago. When he got turned down, he was impossible to work with for a good six months. He's never been the same since."

"So status, more than money."

"Do you ever see a theft motive entirely independent of money, Detective?" she inquired, amused. "Conservators don't get paid particularly well, so I'm sure the financial rewards came into it, as well."

Mason gave a brisk nod. "Well, we'll do what we can. You understand, I've got people looking for him, but it's not like he's a murderer. And a guy like this might very well have planned for getting caught eventually."

"You think he's gone," she said, looking at him steadily.

"I think it's a possibility. We'll do what we can. At this point, we don't know that his alleged forgeries extended beyond the statue that you and Mr. Spencer discovered. And, of course, there's the matter of corrupted evidence. Officially, I should remind you that amateur detective work is bad news. Even if we find Wingate, I'm not at all sure how much of the material you've unearthed will be admissible in court. Mr. Spencer should never have broken into the office or the desk."

"If it hadn't been for Alex, Paul Wingate would have gotten away with stealing a half-million-dollar statue,"

Julia said tartly. And flushed. Where the hell, she wondered, had that come from? "Under the circumstances," she continued more moderately, "we did what we thought was best."

"I understand. That was on the record. Off the record, I think you two did a hell of a job." For the first time, she saw a flicker of humor in Mason's eyes.

"Bunnie Bernaldo," Julia said suddenly.

He gave her a puzzled look. "What?"

"That's where I know you from. Last month, at one of her parties. You were with Cass Richards."

And a bright smile lit up his face, utterly confounding her. "I still am," he assured her. "I still am."

"AND IF YOU THINK of anything else or hear of anything else, please call me right away," Sam Mason finished as he escorted Julia to the door that led to the waiting area and shook her hand. "Thanks for coming in. Please thank Mr. Spencer for me, too."

Julia opened her mouth to say she probably couldn't do that, but the detective was already gone. She started down the hall. Three o'clock, she thought, glancing at the clock on the wall. She'd worn the better part of the day away sitting in offices, telling her tale. Now, finally, she was free to go home. She could brush her teeth, she thought, take a shower, do all the things that she'd fantasized about over the weekend.

Alone. *Alex...* she thought, and waited to see what feelings bubbled up. There was still anger, and loss, and self-recrimination, but the balance had shifted subtly over the course of the day. In the hours that had ensued since Paul Wingate's early-morning visit, she'd had the sneaking suspicion that maybe she'd overreacted.

He'd gone into Paul's office, she reminded herself.

He'd broken into the desk when he'd specifically promised her he wouldn't. He'd broken his word. On the other hand, he'd only done it once he'd discovered the real statue was at risk, and done it because Paul was coming into the lab and he didn't have a choice.

But now Paul was gone, escaped precisely because of Alex's showboating. Then again, given the way their morning had played out, Alex was right—Paul would very likely have escaped long before they'd managed to convince security to detain him. The only real difference in the outcome, now that she thought about it, was that the museum still had the statue, whereas otherwise it would have been out of the country by now.

All things considered, Alex had been something of a hero.

All things considered, Julia had been something of a horse's ass.

She made a noise of frustration and started down the hall to the waiting room.

All things considered, she owed Alex an apology. Not that he probably wanted to hear it from her, after the way she'd treated him. She'd deal with it tomorrow. First things first, she'd get home, brush her teeth—bliss— take a shower, sleep until she woke up.

And maybe call Alex that night, just to get it over with. But the toothbrush, shower, and bed experience were crucial. At least the toothbrush and the shower. Maybe she'd do that, then call him, then sleep.

Or, she thought, fumbling for her cell phone, she could just—

Walk across the waiting room and tap him on the shoulder.

Alex sat in the corner, head tipped back against the

wall, eyes closed. He looked rumpled and exhausted, jaw dark with a three-day beard, circles under his eyes. He could have been home hours before. He'd stayed, she realized, stunned.

He'd stayed for her.

She crossed the room to stand next to him and swallowed. Tap him on the shoulder? Sit beside him? Say his name? Tentatively, she reached out a hand just as a couple of uniformed cops came out the door she'd just left, honking in laughter. Alex started, eyes opening, turning to look at the source of the noise. Turning to look at her.

And he smiled, making Julia's heart do a lazy flip-flop.

"Hey," he said.

She moistened her lips. "Hey, yourself. What are you doing here?"

He sat up and scrubbed his hands through his hair. "I figured I'd wait for you, make sure everything came out okay. I take it everything did?"

"All done." She held out her wrists. "The handcuffs didn't even leave a mark, look."

"Wow, that ten-year sentence went by quick."

"They gave me time off for good behavior. Speaking of which…"

"Yeah?"

She took a glance around, noticing the handful of people waiting. "Can we go outside?"

"Sure." He rose and they began walking to the exit. Outside, the afternoon was warm, with a light breeze sending clouds scudding across an impossibly blue sky. Alex stopped. "Okay. So what did you want to say?"

She took a breath. "I owe you an apology about this morning. I'm sorry I flew off the handle and accused you of…"

"Oh, crimes of state? Babynapping? Consorting with wild animals?"

She flushed. "Look, I've had time to cool down and think about it and I realize that you did what you had to do. I wish it hadn't worked out that way, but the museum's better off for it."

He looked at her steadily, not saying anything.

"I shouldn't have lost my temper. You didn't deserve it. I was just worried about everything and upset and I didn't understand what had happened. I should have listened better." She paused expectantly. Why didn't he say something, dammit? Was it possible he was still furious with her? Was it possible he'd actually been hanging around for some totally different reason? "Anyway," she blurted, "I'm an idiot and I apologize. But I'm sure you want to get home so I'll, um, I'll just get out of your hair now and let you—"

"The hell you will," he said. "Why do you think I stayed?"

"Oh, well, I didn't—"

"I was waiting for you." He caught at her hands and turned her toward him. "To try to talk one more time. I feel like crap about what happened in the lab. I hated going against my word like that, I hated it, but I felt like it was the only choice I had. I know this sounds ridiculous after what's just happened, but under normal circumstances, when I give my word, I keep it."

"I know that," she said, realizing that as she said it, she did. "I learned a few things this weekend, Alex. About myself and about you. I've made assumptions about who you are and they were wrong. It's time to throw them all out and focus on learning who you really are. And I'm wondering...."

"Yes?" His eyes were nearly incandescent.

"I'm wondering if you meant some of the things you said last night. About us."

His eyes were steady. "I meant them. Did you?"

"Yes, I did. But I'm thinking now that what we really need to do is just start all over. From the beginning. No assumptions, no biases, just you and me, taking each other at face value, like we've never met before."

"I'd be happy to take you at face value," he said, looking her up and down, "but it's what's behind the face I'm most interested in."

Julia swallowed and stuck out her hand. "I'm Julia Covington. Nice to meet you."

"I'm Alex Spencer," he said, taking her hand in his.

"I don't suppose by any chance you'd like to go get some coffee, would you?" she asked him.

He laughed and pulled her into his arms. "I'd love to."

Epilogue

RAIN STREAKED THE WINDOWS of the car as it lurched over potholes and uneven pavement. The road—if you could call it that, was unmarked and dark; no one worried about streetlights, not here where the only after-dark pedestrians were the security guards who walked the wharves. Beyond, over on the water, the shadowy bulk of freighters rose like ghost ships in the night.

They were far from the fashionable addresses, with their glossy tenants and glossier rents. This stretch of waterfront was strictly utilitarian. Oil slicked the dark water, a toxic soup perfumed with the twin stenches of diesel fuel and rotting fish.

Allard sat in the backseat, the taste of hopelessness gritty in his mouth. Plastic zip strips bound his wrists and ankles. Renouf's men sat in the front seat, the tall one looking back with the gun to cover him. There would be no escape from these men, he understood that now.

Just as the mouse, long ago, had in the end succumbed to the cobra, so, too, he would succumb.

As they turned the final corner, he saw the gleam of

eyes staring at him from beside a pile of rubbish. A cat, crouched in the night, eyes red in the reflected light.

And in a kind of helpless resignation, Jean Luc Allard was about to meet his doom.

* * * * *

Don't miss the next amazing story in
THE WHITE STAR *continuity...*
INTO TEMPTATION
by award-wining author Jeanie London.
Available April 2006!

If you enjoyed what you just read,
then we've got an offer you can't resist!

Take 2 bestselling
love stories FREE!

Plus get a FREE surprise gift!

Clip this page and mail it to Harlequin Reader Service®

IN U.S.A.	IN CANADA
3010 Walden Ave.	P.O. Box 609
P.O. Box 1867	Fort Erie, Ontario
Buffalo, N.Y. 14240-1867	L2A 5X3

YES! Please send me 2 free Harlequin Temptation® novels and my free surprise gift. After receiving them, if I don't wish to receive anymore, I can return the shipping statement marked cancel. If I don't cancel, I will receive 4 brand-new novels each month, before they're available in stores. In the U.S.A., bill me at the bargain price of $3.80 plus 25¢ shipping and handling per book and applicable sales tax, if any*. In Canada, bill me at the bargain price of $4.47 plus 25¢ shipping and handling per book and applicable taxes**. That's the complete price and a savings of 10% off the cover prices—what a great deal! I understand that accepting the 2 free books and gift places me under no obligation ever to buy any books. I can always return a shipment and cancel at any time. Even if I never buy another book from Harlequin, the 2 free books and gift are mine to keep forever.

142 HDN DZ7U
342 HDN DZ7V

Name _____ (PLEASE PRINT)

Address _____ Apt.#

City _____ State/Prov. _____ Zip/Postal Code

Not valid to current Harlequin Temptation® subscribers.

Want to try two free books from another series?
Call 1-800-873-8635 or visit www.morefreebooks.com.

* Terms and prices subject to change without notice. Sales tax applicable in N.Y.
** Canadian residents will be charged applicable provincial taxes and GST.
  All orders subject to approval. Offer limited to one per household.
  ® are registered trademarks owned and used by the trademark owner and or its licensee.

TEMP04R   ©2004 Harlequin Enterprises Limited

HARLEQUIN®

Blaze™

COMING NEXT MONTH

#243 OBSESSION Tori Carrington
Dangerous Liaisons, Bk. 2
Anything can happen in the Quarter.... Hotel owner Josie Villefranche knows that better than most. Ever since a woman was murdered in her establishment, business has drastically declined. She's very tempted to allow sexy Drew Morrison to help her take her mind off her troubles—until she learns he wants much more than just a night in her bed....

#244 WHAT HAVE I DONE FOR ME LATELY? Isabel Sharpe
It's All About Attitude
Jenny Hartmann's sizzling bestseller *What Have I Done for Me Lately?* is causing an uproar across the country. And now Jenny's about to take her own advice—by having a sexual fling with Ryan Masterson. What Jenny isn't prepared for is that the former bad boy is good in bed—and even better at reading between the lines!

#245 SHARE THE DARKNESS Jill Monroe
FBI agent Ward Cassidy thinks Hannah Garret is a criminal. And Hannah suspects Ward is working for her ex-fiancé, the man who now wants her dead. But when Hannah and Ward get caught for hours in a hot, darkened elevator, the sensual pull of their bodies tells them all they *really* need to know....

#246 MIDNIGHT OIL Karen Kendall
After Hours, Bk. 1
It's the trendiest salon in Miami...and landlord Troy Barrington is determined to shut it down. As part owner and massage therapist, Peggy Underwood can't let him—and his ego—win. So she'll use all of the sensual, er, *spa* tools at her disposal to change his mind.

#247 AFTERNOON DELIGHT Mia Zachary
Rei Davis is a tough-minded judge who wishes someone could see her softer side. Chris London is a lighthearted matchmaker who wishes someone would take him seriously. When Rei walks into Lunch Meetings, the dating service Chris owns, and the computer determines that they're a perfect match, sparks fly! But will all their wishes come true?

#248 INTO TEMPTATION Jeanie London
The White Star, Bk. 4
It's the sexiest game of cat and mouse she's ever played. MI6 agent Lindy Gardner is determined to capture Joshua Benedict—and the stolen amulet in his possession. The man is leading her on a sensual chase across two continents that will only make his surrender oh, so satisfying.